Read by Dawn
Volume Three

Read by Dawn
Volume Three

edited by Adèle Hartley

First published 2008.

Published by Bloody Books®.

9 8 7 6 5 4 3 2 1

Contents

The Last Ditch, *Scott Stainton Miller*   1

Bony Park, *Michael Keyton*   4

Sonny Boy, *Vanessa H. Reid*   9

Dead Frogs, *Josh Reynolds*   26

Treats, *Samuel Minier*   34

What Will Happen When You Are Gone?, *Jeffory Jacobson*   37

A Different Kind Of Sunshine, *Peter Gutiérrez*   56

Swept Away, *Samuel Minier*   69

Septophobia, *Simon Nightingale*   71

Shuck, *Rebecca Lloyd*   77

Chinese Graveyard, *Joel A. Sutherland*   92

Them Potions I drank, *Brian Rosenberger*   104

In the Cinema Tree with Orbiting Heads, *Kek-W*   106

Wendy, *Ryan Cooper*   115

Extensions, *Andrew Tisbert*   126

Murder for Breakfast, *Oren Shafir*   138

Blind Spot, *Jamie Killen*   140

Dawn, *Morag Edward*   150

The Devil's Tavern, *Alison J. Littlewood*   159

Tinsel, *Frazer Lee*   167

Sighs, *Patricia MacCormack*   172

She, *Brian G. Ross*   191

The Wait, *Scott Stainton Miller*   193

Lost, *Sam Thewlis*   206

Keeping Someone, *Samuel Minier*   211

Windchimes, *Paul Kane*   213

Coming to a Close, *Aurelio Rico Lopez III*   234

The Pain of Others, *David Wesley Hill*   238

The Last Ditch

Scott Stainton Miller

When they found her body it would be blue and flecked with dirt. Her belly would be whorled with veins, cold and still with stopped blood. The expression on her face...well, he didn't know. He could only speculate. Maybe it would be peaceful, maybe not. Stephen's mind loaded up on the details and he turned the key in the ignition. The car came to life and it was a good five minutes before he realised it was running.

His wife opened the passenger door and sat down beside him. He felt his blood rise.

She touched his arm with the lightness of an insect and he withdrew inwardly. He looked at her, unable to understand quite how she had managed to create such revulsion. Each day he felt sick, sick at the core. Perhaps, in some small way, he too could be held accountable for this disgust. Perhaps some of it was his doing. He dismissed this. No. It was not him. It was her.

It was all *her*.

The car started up, he checked the rising exhaust

fumes in the rear mirror, his eyes quick like a bird's and as black. He was not still and had not been for a long time now, for maybe a year, maybe for more than a year. It seemed like he'd been planning this trip for as long.

'Where are we going?' she asked.

'I thought maybe into the country.'

'Oh...' He turned to her, his eyes no longer on the road, foot hard against the pedal.

'What do you mean 'oh'?' he asked.

'Nothing.'

'You meant something, you did not mean nothing.'

She swallowed. 'It's just, we didn't bring any food or anything. A blanket even.'

He turned back to the road. He could hear her heart beating over his own.

'We won't need any of those things,' he said quietly and she looked at him puzzled.

'I thought...'

'You thought what?'

'Maybe there would be food, I don't know,' she mumbled.

She shrugged and reached over to stroke his face and he recoiled. She drew back, hurt and a little afraid. For the rest of the trip she was as silent as he was.

The car pulled up at the edge of the forest he had scouted. It was far from anywhere, ugly black and ragged. Nobody in their right mind would come here to walk or spend the day; it would be empty.

It *was* empty, but for them.

'It isn't very nice is it?' she asked, attempting a laugh

that was supposed to convey amused surprise, anything to make him smile or warm to her, but nothing did any more. When he suggested this trip she thought perhaps the disgust he displayed towards her, towards everything it seemed, had receded a little. Perhaps, she had thought, they would have a nice day together. But he showed no signs of warmth or enthusiasm. He was cold as the out-lying dirt.

They stepped from the car and walked through the woods. He was growing more agitated the further they went, his fists opening and closing and opening and closing, until finally he stopped and said 'Here.'

'What?'

'Here,' he said and smiled at her; it had been so long since he'd smiled. It was terrifying, his eyes were bulging out of their sockets, he wasn't blinking. He grabbed her and turned her around.

'Stephen...' she whispered.

'Shhh,' he said.

He pulled their baby daughter out from the harness she wore and laid her naked on the hillside. She wriggled around and began to cry at the shock of the cold.

'I thought we were going to give her food, a blanket.'

'What for?'

She shrugged.

They walked back to the car in silence.

Bony Park

Michael Keyton

'**A**re you sure this is the best spot, Rick?' Robert had serious doubts; he looked up at the sun and then at the steely surface of the lake.

'Why, what's wrong with it?' The younger boy sounded defensive.

'Oh, nothing... It's just that – well it's pretty hot now and likely it'll get hotter and there's not much shade here.'

Rick nodded and looked around. Robert was right of course. Worse than that, they were close to the path, and there was a bench nearby. 'It'll be busy later on, what with zimmies.'

'And joggers.'

'Winos... Thing is, do we take the tent or leave it here?'

Robert sighed. 'I don't know, let me think.' In the cool twilight of the previous evening they had picked what seemed to be a good spot, their tent sheltered by bushes in a small but natural bay. Now it was evident they'd made a strategic mistake. They were just too close to the path. Serious fishing would be out of the question.

Robert looked behind him. It was still early in the morning and the path was already occupied.

A middle-aged man was turning the corner. He carried a paper in his hand. He was smiling. The crunch of gravel grew louder, its rhythm remorseless.

'Morning, boys.' It was a cheery voice, the voice of a man pleased with himself, pleased with the day. He waggled his paper – 'Beautiful morning' – and walked on by.

'Morning.' Robert smiled automatically and stared at the silent water. This was the wrong spot.

Rick grunted, then – 'Wanker.' The sound was barely audible. The man stopped and turned around.

'You're in the wrong spot, you know.' Pleasantly, as if it didn't really matter, but there it was. He paused and wiped his brow with the hand holding the paper.

'Over there,' he said, pointing to a small wooded headland to their right. 'Small cove, just like this, but shaded, that's where you'll find the fish. Used to go there myself – when I was a young'un.' He looked round dubiously and pursed his lips as if in thought. 'Picnics and barbecues by lunch time, on a day like this – screaming children all over the place. Fish? You'll be reeling up toddlers!'

The boys laughed. 'I've never gutted a toddler,' Rick said.

'What about the tent?' Robert glanced sideways at the taut blue fabric, quivering in the early morning breeze.

'Leave it.'

'Can't do that. It's not ours. Anything could happen.'

The three of them studied the tent in silence. The man coughed sympathetically.

'You're right. Can't just leave it, especially if it doesn't belong to you. Look, I'll tell you what, it's on my way. I live just past the gate.' He pointed to a distant glint of metal, the chimneys of some newly built houses fragmented by trees. 'How about I show you the place, and if it's as good as I say it is, well then move camp. It'll be worth it, I'm telling you, boys. Wasting your time in a spot like this... unless you want tiddlers and chips.'

'Toddlers,' Robert shouted.

'Toddlers to you, too!' the man chuckled.

'You go, I'll guard the tent.' Rick started reeling in his line. 'Call me if it's any good.'

Robert nodded and stepped onto the path alongside the stranger. 'Is that the paper, there?'

The man looked at his paper and then at Robert. His eyes twinkled behind glasses. 'Yes,' he said.

'What I mean is does it have last night's score?'

'United? Yes, I suppose so. Here, take it.' The two of them ambled along the path towards where the fishing was better. Robert, immersed in the back pages, stumbled several times. He was jabbering in excitement, or indignation. The man didn't appear to be listening. Rick looked at them until they turned the corner and made a decision. Any place had to be better than this. He'd get the tent packed in readiness.

'There you go.' The man's voice was calm.

Robert squinted at the bushes.

'The path's just beyond. Look, you can see the lake

from here.' Robert stared over the gleaming foliage. Just beyond was water, a shimmering tongue poking into a dense cluster of willow and ash. The man pointed with his paper towards the gate. 'Right, I'll be off, then.'

Robert hesitated.

A crunch of gravel. A smile. Followed by a tap on the head with the newspaper. 'Come on then, follow me.' The man sounded resigned.

The two of them pushed through the bushes, displacing sunlight and green metallic-looking leaves.

They stopped on a thin strand of gravel and sand. A gloved hand wrapped itself around Robert's throat; fingers, lean brown hands, worrying, shaking, digging their way deeper into his flesh. The lake, pale and sparkling, blurred into a bluish smear. The boy's legs lost contact with the ground, a mountainous weight fell upon him, and his face smacked into gravel.

The man looked down upon him in quiet anticipation. Where to make the first cut? He knelt, scrutinising the boy's neck. There – just below the ear, a small mole. Still uncertain, his knife hand moved downwards, pushing a small dark curl out of the way. He had to be certain. It had to feel right. Be right. Thumb and forefinger touched the mole, almost tenderly, stretching the skin in readiness for the first cut. *Ohh yes! Do it... Do it – do it – do it.* The voice was urgent, impatient.

Robert opened his eyes. His lips widened into what would have been a scream.

The sign! A change of target. Steel, finely honed and shining, rammed into the boy's open mouth, slicing savagely this way and that, pressing right the way down until the point scraped against bone. It felt right. He grabbed the boy's hand.

Rick was sweating, his shirt wet and sticky, clinging to his back. Every part of him prickled, and his head felt heavy with heat. A headache was coming, either that or a storm, or both. Every so often, he shaded his eyes and stared down the path. In his mind, he saw a cool, tree-shadowed cove, and he wondered why Robert was taking so long. But the job was done. Tent neatly packaged with rods firmly attached. In the distance, he heard a faint shout. A man was waving a newspaper at him.

He picked up the tent and rods and trotted eagerly along the path.

Sonny Boy

Vanessa H. Reid

S he wrung her wrinkled hands in tiny, close movements and stared out the front window. For the third time that afternoon, she searched the sleepy street outside for any sign of her youngest son's return. *It's getting so late. Where is he?* Her mind narrowly skirted panic as she reminded herself that he was all right; they didn't know that he did it. And if they did find out? Well, she would make sure he was all right. They weren't going to take her little boy. He didn't mean to. He was not himself that night. He was so sorry. She knew. A mother knows.

'You sure he's coming tonight?' hollered Father from the kitchen. His voice rumbled through the hall and rattled the miniature china service that he had brought back from Japan. She winced. His voice carried accusation even when he was just asking about the weather. 'You know how you hear what you want to sometimes, Mother. 'Cause it suits you.' She could smell his freshly lit cigarette. Pale smoke slunk through the halls. It lived in the fabric of the house.

'Yes! He's coming,' she moaned back as she had for

fifty-one years. Her tone always carried grief, even when she told him the weatherman said sun. 'I know it. I heard them say it. They believed him. That he didn't do it. They said he was coming back Friday to get a few things and not to leave town. He's coming.' *I know he is.* Mother looked down at her hands wrestling like sightless baby birds, fingers crawling blindly over one another and she managed to pull them apart. Suddenly, she felt a little off. She reached up and grasped the heavy brocade curtains in an effort to steady herself. She needed to leave the parlour. She was making herself half crazy. *Go back in the kitchen and finish supper, woman.* Her little boy would be home soon and he would need to eat. How frightened he must be.

She remembered bringing that baby boy home. Father was away on business – just like with her oldest son. Her neighbour Ollie was there watching Junior and her own mother helped her up the stony steps of the front porch. She held fast to that squirmy bundle. He was so warm, all movement and agitation. Like a puppy. He was always restless. Even in her belly he turned and kicked and pushed. And he rarely slept. God, he made her so sick. She was sick for nine months and even after; she didn't recover well from the caesarean section. She still had a waxy, craggy scar across her dough-bag belly. That day though, she felt no pain. Nothing. She walked up those steps so carefully. It was cold. Hard cold that rarely came that far south. She remembered feeling the frozen porch steps through the soles of her shoes. It felt like walking on a tomb.

She made it as far as that very parlour before she had to sit down. She sat right there, on the formal sofa. Now it was so faded but then it was practically new. Father got a great deal. It was a high quality piece, he said. Got the best deal because of his connections, he said. They loved him at the Macon store. She remembered looking down next to her knees and following the vined pattern as it scrolled and weaved to the armrest and, for a moment, she was lost in it, curling to nothingness. The medicine the nurses gave her took her concentration but the active boy in her lap brought her back to herself. He turned and mewed, eyes red and squinting. He coughed then and his goopy eyes opened widely. She looked into the glassy denim pools and she was lost. He focused on her – even in his first days he could do that – looked deeply into her eyes and saw everything she was, and it was okay. Sonny. He was the first man, besides her daddy, that ever looked at her that way. He saw her weaknesses, her sins. He even saw her virtues – there were more of them then – and he didn't turn away...

Mother blinked at the floor, hands still grasping the cool curtains as she stooped over, pulling the fabric panels down with her memories. Their relationship had never been sweeter than that moment when she brought him home, but they had a few nice ones after that. Mostly, it was his promise – his potential – that kept her viewing him as that squeaky, red-eyed mass of warm, jerky movement. She just couldn't see past that and never would. No matter what they said he did. They always lied about her boy.

'MOTHER!' Father bellowed. 'If he comes tonight like you say he is, he won't come in if he sees you there. You know that, don't you? Damn it! We're the last people he wants to see right now. Get in this kitchen – Now! I'm so damned tired of saying it.' She could hear him strike the match and suck hard. He was lighting another one. She listened to his cool, lingering inhale and she knew he didn't want it to end. She could tell that like all *his* things, he didn't want it to end. The problem – yes, she was aware of it – was that it all does end. He either didn't or couldn't believe it. Or maybe he just wouldn't, she thought. *He thinks he's so smart.* He thought he was much smarter than she was. Even though he cursed like the white trash that used to live down on the corner of her daddy's farm. Her husband had no excuse. He went to college. He was from a good family. Now he just sat and smoked and cursed like white trash.

Mother sighed deeply as if all the sorrows of the past rode out on her breath and sprinkled to the floor around her feet. There wasn't much time. She straightened herself upright and closed the curtains; the now dusky light dulled except for a thin line that glowed through the folds. In the shadows of her front parlour, where she once entertained the former mayor and his second wife and they ruled her baked artichoke dip *the best in the county*, she turned and walked wordlessly to the kitchen; her hands rejoined in front of her in their twisting, anxious flutter.

'Son of a bitch!' Father hissed under his breath. He said it often. It was more of a tic than a statement. SONOFABITCH. Smoke circled his face in sightless rolls and waves like white worms crawling up his cheeks, down his ears. He inhaled his failing Winston, held on, and then reluctantly let go in a release of smoke and dark thoughts. He was at the end and thought about dragging on the filter but put it out instead. He scratched the butt against the powdery remains in the ashtray and felt the old Formica table's comforting wobbles with each stub, stub, stub. He wouldn't light another for a while. Mother was coming down the hall to finish supper and she hated it when he smoked while she cooked. He usually went out back but it was too hot. Also, Junior, his oldest boy, was back there on the porch stewing in his own anger. Father didn't want any part of that. Not right now. He watched a fat, black fly bump endlessly against the inside of the hazy window. The kitchen wasn't much better but it got the least amount of sun during the day so here he was. Waiting.

He watched Mother come in, hands twisting again. With a mix of tenderness and revulsion, he watched her shuffle to the stove to stir the pot. What had happened to his girl? She was so pretty, so bright once. Now, she was sad. Sad all over. In her profile, he occasionally saw that sweet little girl. In her small, upturned nose. Her high cheekbones that got her second and third looks from the fellows at the drug store. Boy, how his cronies envied him in the old days. Seymour Groverdale promised to steal her away if he wasn't careful. She was the prettiest thing at the dances. The loveliest woman at the conventions. The former mayor even had an eye for her. *Bastard.* Father watched him closely. Everyone knew how he got re-elected. Not to mention how he got all of those wives.

Now Father just sat still, watched Mother cook, and waited for his youngest son to come home. He thought about him again. He'd been thinking about him off and on most of the day. Father wasn't sure what he felt about what happened. Anger. Sadness. The worst part was that he wasn't surprised. He didn't know why. What his son did was terrible. Father just wasn't surprised, somehow. A father knows what his children are capable of. That's the joy and defeat of it. With his youngest, he thought there'd be more joy. There was some.

He remembered that day, the day Sonny had come home from college. He was a Valdosta State man, just like himself. It was the end of his boy's first semester and they all waited in the parlour for him to drive up. Mother had made a big supper that caused his belly to grumble just thinking of it. The smells in the house brought Father home when he was thinking about going elsewhere on more than one occasion. His oldest son, Junior, was even there. They were all waiting for the golden boy's return. They were waiting for the stories – the challenges, the triumphs of which he was sure to tell. He could tell a yarn and keep everyone in the room from breathing.

Finally, Sonny pulled up in his red convertible. Father was looking out the window and saw his son's expression, pinched and tired. As his boy walked reluctantly to the front stoop, he stopped and saw his father in the window. The younger man shifted his expression and smiled. Once he threw open the door, his voice was already going, 'Aw, hell, everybody! I didn't know you'd make such a fuss for this old college man!' Mother ran to him and embraced her little boy. His older brother held back, sipping a Jack and Coke and working a wry smile. As Mother fawned and mewled, Sonny looked up at his father hesitantly. Father smiled, clapped him solidly on his slender shoulder, and shook him hard.

'All right boy, let's hear all about it,' Father grinned.

The family moved in to the kitchen as the boy told of making contacts, making the dean's list, and – on the side – told his Father about making at least ten women scream his name. 'That's my boy, Sonny,' Father thought. It wasn't until the following week that Father got a call from the Dean of Students. Mr. Johnston T. Rockingham told Father that his youngest son was being asked to leave Valdosta State, his own Alma Mater. Something about inappropriate behaviour, academic dishonesty, and even a suggestion of drug use. Father hung up on the dean, SONOFABITCH, and he and Sonny never spoke of the matter. What was there to say? He knew the girl part must be true. His youngest took after him in that way. *Good lookin' fucker.*

The memory was strangely sweet. Yes, there was some joy. But it was infected with this human truth that he couldn't quite understand and, as far as he knew, couldn't be fixed. At least he had never thought of any way. And he had tried. They all had. But what to do about this new situation. Father wasn't sure as he looked out the back window at the dying summer sun while the fat, black fly just bumped blindly against the glass.

The back door moaned on its hinges as Junior opened it up to the kitchen. 'Shit! It's hotter than hell out there,' he said as he stomped down the curling vinyl tile that usually caught the door. He managed to dislodge it completely anyway and slammed the door shut in frustration. 'Is that rat bastard here yet?'

'Junior!' Mother said.

'SONOFABITCH,' said Father. 'Now that's enough out of you. I've got all I need right now without you giving me some kind of shit. And don't get Mother upset. We don't need that either.'

Junior paled, stricken. He blinked at his father. After what his little brother had done, after all the pain he had caused the family, Father yelled at *him*. After Junior had quit college and gone into the family business when Daddy got sick. *Fuckin' bastard*. After years of lies, humiliation, and near financial ruin all at the hands of his brother, Father still loved Sonny the best and would rather sit and wait for him to come home than go on. *AFTER WHAT HE'D JUST DONE?!* Father watched as Junior's startled face smoothed briefly to sadness and then began to crease into brittle lines of a tiny hatred. Father turned away from him.

Junior glanced at his mother and saw her pity. It wouldn't help. He frowned deeply, jowls tucking in, baring his teeth like a cornered bulldog. He pounded out of the kitchen down the hall, through the parlour, slamming out the front door with his fists clenched. As the screen porch door sung low to a quiet close on its pressurised hinge, Junior heard his father yell, 'Don't you stay out there long, you hear?! He'll see you!' *Son of a bitch.* Junior glanced over at the gentle swaying porch swing, breathed deeply, and felt his anger ebb a little. He sat down on its green, chipped slats as he had done so many times before and just swung back and forth, back and forth. As he expected, he relaxed with each pump of his legs and listened as the chains sighed and creaked reassuringly. That's when he thought about it. He thought about that night.

He had been sitting out on the porch just like this. It was a similarly hot evening but so humid. He felt drops of sweat pop out around his brow. They would meet and mingle and then ride down his cheeks like a woman's slow caress. There were no clouds that night, not one. He remembered looking up at the studded sky, watching the stars wink and flicker. He was just nineteen and making a life changing decision. His daddy had cancer. He couldn't work for a while, and 'Need you to come to the store for a while and help out, buddy. Know I can count on you. Will you do it?' Junior pretended to mull it over but they both knew he wasn't going back to school. He would do what Father asked. Fuck. Junior hunched over, pressing his face into his hands and bobbed up and down between his knees. Then he heard his brother's car glide down their side street and turn into the driveway.

Junior sat up and watched his baby brother struggle out of the car and wobble up the pavement, stopping and starting and grinning like an ass, all the while. Drunk. He was drunk and probably more. Junior sighed. Probably say it was because of Father. Jesus.

'Hell-ooo there, big brother,' he said gaily. 'Looking at the stars, are you?' Sonny made a misstep onto the porch and fell to one knee, grabbing the railing and chuckling. If Junior was drunk as well, God that he was, he'd be laughing at himself too, he thought. Instead of standing up, his little brother plopped down onto the top step and looked at Junior. His smiled faded.

'So, you taking over the ol' business?'

'I'm not taking over shit,' he said. 'Father just needs some help, that's all. Soon as he's back on his feet, I'm going back to Valdosta. Soon as he's well, I mean.'

The younger brother blinked at Junior with a bleary gaze, his head swaying slightly snake-like, his teeth flashed, 'You lie.'

Junior, startled, stared back. 'What did you say?'

'You are a liar. You think I'm stupid? You're here for good and you are going to sit right under our daddy's wing and whisper in his ear, strokin' his feathers. 'Good birdie.' That's what you're going do. You'll climb up 'im, perch on his shoulder, and tell him all about it until he dies. Then, you're going to be the big man and tell us all what to do. That's what'll happen, so don't you lie to me,' he spat. 'You always whisper and poison, whisper and poison till no one wants me. Well, I've got news for you big brother – someone wanted me. Someone wanted me real bad. I've been fucking your girl. Donna said we had to keep it quiet. Didn't you wonder why she broke up with you like that? She didn't want you to know. But it doesn't matter now. I'm done with your old pussy. She even got herself pregnant. Ha! Might have been mine... hell, it might have been yours. Like the world needs another Varner man. I made her get rid of that shame. Told her I'd tell you. She begged me not to leave, but I was done. Now, what do you think about that big brother?'

In a single movement, Junior lit from the swing, straddled his brother, and raised a coiled fist to his face. He pounded and pounded with a sick smacking sound until his knuckles began to slip on the blood and ooze that ran from his brother's nose. 'Come on, brother. You've been wanting to do this for a long time,' Sonny lisped wetly. Junior drove down on his brother over and over. He could feel the bones in his brother's face. They felt like sticks of blackboard chalk grinding down with each slam, slam. Junior stopped, fist in mid-air, when he realised that Sonny wasn't fighting back; he wasn't even blocking the blows. Junior relaxed his thighs, stared down at his little brother, and waited for him to say something.

'Don't stop,' Sonny whispered wetly through blood-sticky lips. He coughed and looked at his brother through one squinted eye. 'Please just...kill me. Oh, God please.'

Then, Junior saw it. He saw just how broken and

bent Sonny was. How he always had been. He saw that his brother was a tragic man but that he loved him no matter what. Loved him more than anything. He couldn't help it, even when he wanted him to die. Sonny lost his hollow look and began a slow grin, 'What are you going to do, kiss me you asshole?' Junior smiled back and the two boys chuckled softly into the moist, summer night.

Junior remembered himself and sat up in the swing when he heard a car coming up the main street. He knew it was his brother without even looking. He scrambled to his feet and slipped inside the front door, pulling it closed behind him. He looked out the window and saw that it was indeed his brother coming home. Sonny drove his old truck slowly, cautiously onto their street. Junior could only make out the outline of his head behind the windshield in the blackening night. 'He's here,' he said as he rushed down the hall to the kitchen to alert his parents. 'He's here.' He looked at Father. 'What'd you decide?'

Father looked up at him and hesitated for a moment. 'He can stay.' Mother whimpered in relief. Junior stiffened but nodded.

'All right, Father. Whatever you say.'

Mother and Junior eased around the kitchen table. Mother sunk down next to Father while Junior sat at the end of the table and waited.

No one's here. Sonny paused at the bottom of the front porch steps and looked up. His skeletal frame and greying skin made him look fifty-five – not forty-five. He frowned and scratched at the open sore on his cheek. He had picked it open so much, now it wouldn't heal. *I've got to go in. Got to do it. Just get my stuff and get out. I can do this.*

Sonny took one soft step at a time, lingering on each until he shuffled onto the porch. He stood there for a moment. He hadn't been back since that night and it felt sickeningly similar. Maybe time hadn't passed. Maybe he was still here. He rubbed his weary eyes in the hope that the scene would change. It did not. The only difference was the broken police tape that hung over the railing. *Someone hadn't taken that down?* He watched its jagged tail flutter slightly even though there wasn't a breeze. He still couldn't remember what happened that night. When he slept, if he could, he thought he saw the events in snapshots. Lurid photographs he could not believe. SNAP. They appeared behind his eyes and he couldn't look away. It was as if he were being held down, his eyelids forced open, and he was made to see the sins of another man.

Like a spectre, Sonny swept across the porch and opened the screen door, careful to avoid anyone's notice. He didn't need that. He turned the front knob; it wasn't locked. He pushed open the door and walked into the parlour, closing the door behind him and looking around the room. The only light was the moonlight that filtered through the front windows and cast a powdery glow on the furniture. It had been the same since he could remember. It smelled lightly of bleach and lilacs – his mother's cleaning formula. Only there was a thin film of dust on the contents of the parlour.

He hesitated and thought about turning down the hall and going to his room. He should just get his stuff and go. *Grab it.* Take that old duffle from his closet, grab his things and go. He should just get away. *Go now! Get out. Get out. Get out!* He twitched. Small town cops. How they believed him, that he didn't do it, that he wasn't there when it happened, he couldn't figure. *Go, go, go!* But, there was something – a glow from the kitchen. An odd, familiar glow. *Was somebody here?* He imagined that he would walk into a comfortable family scene. Just like nothing had happened. He even imagined that he smelled his mother's beef stew. *DT's... Got to be.* The call was too much. Maybe, if he went in he thought, it would be like it was when he was a little boy and the room was warm and beckoning. When life felt safe and before he...before he became himself. Before he knew what his family was. How they would fail him. How they would only be what they were. The need to look overwhelmed him. Sonny turned and walked down the hall to the kitchen. The light. He had to see. He would be careful so no one would see.

Sonny stopped and stood at the threshold of the kitchen. His mouth slackened and he paled at the scene in front of him; bile bubbled up and burned his throat. He swallowed and blinked wildly, rubbing his eyes trying to erase the vision. He could not believe. *Oh, God.* It wasn't so. He saw his mother, his father, and his brother, seated around the kitchen table. All looking up at him expectantly. *They couldn't be...*

He looked at his mother. She stood and searched his eyes for something but his gaze trailed down to the morbid hole in her belly. She stood starkly calm as the gunshot wound to her womb leaked a vile, black tar. It seemed to drip rusty, oozing tears that would disappear. Then it would drip again and repeat without culminating, trickling nowhere. She smiled encouragingly. 'Oh, Sonny. We've been so worried.' Sonny's head jerked back, snapping his neck as the white, harsh memory flashed in his mind, blinding him for a moment. He bit his tongue with the seizure and tasted copper juice in his mouth as the picture came into focus. *SNAP. For a moment he saw his mother that night. In her bed. He raised the gun. BAM! Lying still on her side, lips slightly parted. Facing Father. She never knew it was coming. She never knew it was him. He was grateful for that. SNAP.*

Then Sonny looked at Father. He was the same as he remembered him, only, when he turned his head, Sonny could see straight through the bullet hole in his charred skull. The skin had pulled apart like the rotting rind on an orange, opening to expose pulsating movement and grey nothing – a slippery mass. *SNAP. Sonny looked from his mother's soft repose to his father lying there. He had awakened at the sound and had began to baulk, his eyes wide, his hands held out in front of him. 'Sonny!' But Sonny came close, told his old man to shut up, and then put the gun to his ear and fired without hesitation. BAM! He was out of his mind, after all. SNAP.*

Finally, Sonny looked at Junior. As usual, Junior sat with a look of sullen dissatisfaction, like he might bite if he hadn't been kicked so often. His wound was the worst. He hunched over the table but Sonny could still see the blow to his chest was angry and seeping. Like Mother's wound, it dripped and receded, except *his* guts hung out like oily, twitching snakes. They even pulled horribly inward with Junior's phantasmal pulse. In and out. In and out. *SNAP. Sonny heard his brother coming and ran to meet him in the hallway. 'What the hell?' Junior hollered. Sonny hesitated longer than with his mother and father, but he couldn't stop now. Junior was almost upon him. 'Sonny, what are you doing?' What had begun must end. He was in trouble. He would have shot himself that night but he was too selfish. Even high and mad, he couldn't do it. Now, he didn't want to stop. He knew that meant he was crazy. He knew enough to put the gun where no one would find it. They still hadn't. Crazy. Then, he watched his brother reach out for him in the moonlight and Sonny pulled the trigger. BAM! It was better for everyone. SNAP.*

Sonny returned to himself and trembled. *This isn't real. It can't be! How could...* Finally, Father spoke: 'We've been waiting son. We've been waiting for you. You're home now. It's uh...it's all right,' he said.

Sonny took a step back, held his hands out in front of him, and shook his head in quick, erratic movements. Junior stood up. 'Don't you run. We're here to take you in for good now. We know you've got nowhere. We're your family. You belong here. You know it, don't you?'

Sonny looked at his family and, in his mind, sought to preserve himself as he always had. He took another step back thinking he would turn and leave, never to return. This would go away too. Everything did. Didn't it? He stopped, however, when his mother began to walk toward him. She bowed her lips into a familiar soft smile, tilting her head in that way he knew. Then, she came upon him and raised her arms to reach for him, as if to pull him back into her belly, which was now just a fetid, weepy hole. 'Sonny boy, it's okay. You're here now. Here to stay. We could never let you back out into that world. They don't understand you; but we do. You're home. Welcome home.'

Dead Frogs

Josh Reynolds

Being out in the open on a day like this one was like breathing soup.

Junior Rose wiped at his greasy face with an almost equally greasy rag, his sweat-stained baseball cap hung down by his thigh, the frayed brim clutched between two calloused fingertips. He stood on the left bank of Callygar Road, legs straddling the ditch itself. Across the narrow stretch of gravel road, a corn field sprang up out of the wet ground, green and red and tall. It had been a bad year for corn. Junior was glad to see at least this patch of it doing well. Most of it anyway. The ears closest to the road were dried, brown stalks. Rotting instead of ripening.

The smell of the corn, freshly cut grass and damp earth mingled, sliding through the haze like invisible snakes to tease the nose. Overhead, the sun beat down, steaming light drizzling through the cracks in the closely packed trees and the ugly clouds above them and carrying with it a wet heat that coiled around everything. The air should have been heavy with the hum of frogs;

a plastic sound, like a hundred children's noise-makers all going at once, echoing from every tree.

Instead, it was quiet. Except for the corn shifting and scraping in the warm breeze. Like a voice, just out of the range of his ears.

Opposite the corn field was an empty lot. There had been a house there once. A while back. Now it was weeds and shaggy trees and rotting logs. Callygar Road was a long, twisty, empty stretch of nothing that climbed back up through the bowels of the county like a tapeworm in a dog. One of many empty stretches in this part of the county.

He shook his head and looked up at the swollen clouds in the sky as he pulled his cap back on. Looked like rain. Good. They needed it. His eyes fell back to the ditch running between his legs. Full of black water, the ditch was nearly waist deep and brimming with bright green weeds. There were tree roots growing out of the bank. Mosquitoes hummed through the air, skirting the edges of Junior's vision and darting hungrily at his cheeks, neck and forearms. He batted at them unconsciously and squatted on one edge of the ditch, his fingers trailing through the water, dispersing the slick skin that had formed on top. He rubbed his fingertips together and peered closely at the water.

Frogs floated there. Dozens of them. All dead, pale bellies shining wetly.

They had been reported by a county work crew trimming the ditch banks earlier in the day. A dead frog or two was natural in the ditches. Three dozen however, warranted investigation. Figuring out why they were dead was Junior's job. He'd worked for the Department of Natural Resources for four years and he'd seen the worst South Carolina could throw at someone. Droughts, hurricanes, rabies outbreaks, fire, famine and flood. That was the kind of thing DNR paid him for. Paid him to look in to.

But this? It wasn't the kind of thing you usually saw. At least Junior had never seen it. Not before. Probably wouldn't see it since. At least not belly up like this. Contorted and floating like little rubber toys. He resisted the urge to poke one. He bent slightly, still crouched, using one hand for balance. The water stank of rot and heat this close and he felt the urge to hold his breath. He looked towards one end of the ditch to the other. The drainage pipe openings on either end were obscured by detritus and drooping, yellowed weeds. But still, he could almost make out...

Behind him, the corn whispered again, the breeze ruffling the sweat dampened curls of hair that stuck out from beneath his cap.

Junior sighed and reached around behind himself, pulling a pair of tan work gloves out from his back pocket. He pulled them on with practised ease, letting them snap into place and, still on the edge of the ditch, he crouch-crawled towards the closest of the drainage pipes. Junior chewed his lip for a second. Then he thrust his hand into the pipe, feeling around blindly. Even covered, the skin of his hand prickled as he touched a sodden, hairy mass. With a grunt he dragged it through the sludge and weeds, bringing it into the light of the sun.

The cat stared up at him through glassy eyes, mouth open in a snarl that was forever silent. A muddy, feral calico, rangy and long. Now it was a mass of bones wrapped in skin. Junior examined it with no small amount of disgust. No wounds marked it, as near as he could tell. No broken bones.

He left the cat half floating in the water and stood, looking around. His eyes caught the sparkle of reflected sunlight on the opposite ditch-bank, the one closest to the dead lot. He stepped over the ditch awkwardly, nearly sliding down the muddy bank into the standing water. He dug his fingers into the ground and half-pulled himself up onto the bank. In the weeds, a snake lay dead. It was stretched out, eyes opaque and tinted a murky blue, the sun shining off the black scaled length of it. Just a rat snake. No marks. Dead. Junior looked back at the sodden lump of the cat. Then at the frogs. He shook his head, trying to think.

Poison? Maybe some pesticides got into the ground-water, ran off into the ditch. Cat drank the water and died. Frogs did as well. Maybe the snake ate a frog and died. Junior looked out at the lot, his throat working. He felt slightly sick. This wasn't good. Not at all.

It meant paperwork. A lot of paperwork. If it was poison.

He took a hesitant step onto the lot, gravel and dead leaves crackling under his boots. The lot was a sea of low leaning trees covered in shrivelled bark, their crooked roots protruding from the soil and fallen examples huddled among the sand patches and the yellowed, brittle grass. Dead grass. Just like the weeds. And the trees, come to that. He stepped near the closest one, fingers running over the bark. It smelled foul. A gummy, sour stink coating the skin of it. His touch caused the bark to crumble in places. Junior grabbed a branch, yanking on it. It cracked loudly and came away in his hand. A round mass tumbled toward his head.

'Shit!'

Junior stumbled back, the branch dropping from his hands as he batted wildly at the air around his head. He stepped back, heart jumping in his chest, and stared down at the hornet nest laying quiet and still on the ground at his feet. His eyes narrowed and he squatted, snatching up a stick to jab at the nest, his legs tensing slightly in preparation to leaping up and sprinting for cover. He poked it once. Twice.

It remained silent.

He flicked the stick up and then down, cracking open the nest like an egg. Dead hornets spilled out, a hundred dried little raisins.

Everything was dead here.

Junior closed his eyes and tossed the stick aside. It struck the corpse of a wren with a thump, sending downy feathers spiralling up into the sluggish air. Junior glanced at it and shook his head. His eyes caught a pale flash, piss white.

Bones. Not many. But enough. Bird bones, rat bones, snake bones. Some bigger. He didn't feel like examining them for marks.

There was a smell coming from the dirt, a dark smell

like what was on the trees. The grass too. The weeds. The water in the ditch. He rubbed his fingers together. He could feel it clinging to him through his gloves.

Junior swallowed, the lump that had suddenly appeared in his throat not moving an inch. There was a tiny blossom of pain sitting at the bottom of his head but growing quickly. Climbing up the plates of his skull. He rubbed the back of his head, heedless of the dirt he was coating his neck with. His stomach lurched unpleasantly and he swallowed again, bile trickling down his throat. The sour smell was growing stronger, clinging to him. Wrapping around him.

Poison. Had to be some kind of poison to do all of this. Something in the ground. But whatever it was, was spreading. Growing. The trees further back from the ditch had been dead longer than those closer to the road. Animals too.

He stepped quickly back towards the ditch, where the smell wasn't so bad. His stomach lurched as he moved. He needed to clear his head. Try and figure out what was going on. What had happened here. It wasn't recent. Couldn't be. Not to this extent.

The corn rustled and he stared at it. At the dead, withered stalks closest to the road.

How far had it spread?

His foot caught on something – a root? – and he toppled. He hit the embankment hard, the wind whooshing out of his lungs in a gasp as he slid down towards the water. He scrabbled desperately at the ground, trying to halt his slide. The water between the weeds looked blacker than before. Hungry. Empty but for dead things.

Dead mosquitoes. Dead frogs. Junior's fingers dug inches into the soft, foul soil. His shoulders screamed as he caught himself, his face inches from the water. The weeds tickled his nose.

He stared at the water.

Something stared back, looking up at him through the weeds.

It was a face, or something that was trying to be. A skull of roots and weeds and black things that shone unhappily under the water. Jaws that were little more than gums and teeth made of trash grinned up at him through the oily water as they twisted towards him. It looked bigger than it should beneath the water. Distorted. Bigger than the ditch itself. Junior wanted to scream, but found his mouth too dry to release any sound save a strangled grunt.

Its eyes were dull, the colour of bottled lightning and they flashed as they focused on Junior's own.

He felt sick. Weak. The smell of the water – no, of the thing in the water – grew stronger and stronger, enveloping him like the hands of a giant.

The dirt of the ditch bank under him shifted and he felt himself sliding again. Being pulled along by what he'd assumed were tree roots, but really weren't.

How big was it?

How long had it sat under the dirt, growing? Waiting for its next meal to come along.

The things that weren't roots pulled Junior towards the water, inexorably. Impossibly strong.

It was still hungry.

The water surged up around his face, filling his mouth, his nostrils. He gagged, trying to fight his way free but there was no leverage. He tried again to scream, but the water rushed upwards, filling his throat as he was pulled down, down towards that awful, giant face, towards those hungry, hungry eyes. He was drowning in less than four feet of water.

No. Not drowning.

But dying all the same.

Treats

Samuel Minier

S he lines the children up all down the hallway, parallel with the mouldy stripes festering in the wallpaper. She passes down the row of them, wind-up
soldiers under parade inspection. Inspection's too harsh,
though – really, she's appreciating them. Admiring,
savouring. And not really soldiers – not at attention at
all. Bodies as stable as wobbly wooden nightstands, eyes
wandering motionlessly, swimming from the minty table-
spoon of opium and certain plants collected in her garden
by moonlight.

Some occasionally rise up through the syrup – a
whimper, a finger spasm like a sea critter twitching
through the muck. These ones she lovingly taps with two
fingers on the forehead, her touch a kiss without lips,
dropping them back into fathoms-deep lullaby.

Like a dream for her too, this savoury drifting. Her
hallway is...well, to say it was long would be to say that
drowning is uncomfortable.

When she gets to the very last child, her wrapping
spindle is already waiting. And so the last becomes the

first, and the first is always the hardest, her hands clumsy after three hundred and sixty four spindle-less days. Without the proper cradling motion, the wax paper bunches up in the heavy rollers, and when the elegant, skeletal crimpers clamp the wrapping shut, the child is ill-positioned. An effortless snap, then another less-defined noise, and then a hair tuft oozing from the top of the bundle. This one she regretfully discards – still technically usable, but there is an aesthetic to be considered.

After that, it gets easier – the movements re-acquaint themselves, the spindle strikes up familiar conversations, an old friend both embraced and embracing. She and it work their way back up the hall together with intricate teasings and pulls, a conjoined spider crafting web-globes.

She has five more to wrap when the night just beyond the front door wakes up. Distant whoops like marsh cranes on the wing, called and then gone. And then back. And swelling. Now delicate clicks – claws against cobblestone – and she understands without surprise or anger they're scaling and scampering on the outside of her house. She is crimping the last top when the front door booms with a knock, like Fate itself has grown a fist and come a-callin'.

She beams at the children, their shapes and features translucent beneath the orange and black. Gummy faces, shiny wrappers. A few of them quiver in response to night's breath when she opens the door. It must be the night chill – even the syrup could not keep them still if they could see what waited for them. Waited with billowing burlap sacks.

Or maybe they are quaked by the song, its pitch a tsunami of static as she hands out the first child. The words are alien but the melody is well-known – a tune of threat and reward, and giving something good to eat.

What Will Happen
When You Are Gone?

Jeffory Jacobson

For a confused moment, Katherine was afraid to say something when she finally saw the sign; something fluttered in her throat and crawled up the back of her skull as the letters came into view. Once a heart-stopping neon orange, they were now just the color of old pennies under a wet concrete sky. Katherine could make out the F and O and R and S and A but that was all. A snowdrift obscured the rest. The feeling slipped away and she blurted, 'Is that it?'

Ed stomped on the brakes. The Dodge shuddered as the wheels fought for purchase on asphalt slick with ice. Luckily, no one was behind them. In fact, the entire highway, as far as Katherine could see, was empty.

'One way to find out,' Ed said and followed the two faint ruts of cold earth that lashed through the silent fields of drifting snow. Katherine sighed. This was typical of her husband. There was no stopping and discussing the possibilities that this was the place. Either it was or it wasn't. He plunged ahead to find out, regardless of the consequences.

But he was fearless and he was handsome and he was smart in other ways.

That was enough for Katherine, who had grown up in a tiny rural town in western Kentucky. Ed had been her high school sweetheart, and their marriage had been seemingly predestined from the moment she met him, all the way back in the third grade. She had a sharp, narrow face, and her sarcasm could cut to the bone, but she came across as kind-hearted with a healthy sense of humour at her own expense. Her natural blond hair, split evenly down the middle of her skull, contrasted abruptly with Ed's angry black bristles.

And despite his sometimes thick-headed, flat-out stubbornness, she loved her husband.

That's why she had agreed to accompany him over six hundred miles, up through Indiana, Illinois, and deep into northern Wisconsin, to go investigate what might be a suitable home. She wanted to raise a family and Ed wanted out from under the financial thumbprint of Katherine's father. Ed's brother had inherited the family ranch while Ed worked at the grain store, quietly saving for his own spread.

They'd spent the past two days looking at ranches just out of their price range, seeing if they could get any of the owners to budge. None had. This was the ninth ranch, a place that no real estate agent had ever heard of. All Katherine knew was that Ed had heard about it from a friend, Tom Hunt, a slick guy who always talked Ed into drinking too much when they went out. Supposed to be some kind of ranch, Tom said, way up in the knotted

hills of Iron County. Way, way up north. Nearly fifty per-
cent under the going rate, per acre. The owner was some
lady that had lost her husband and just wanted to move
back to Florida.

'So what's wrong with it?' Ed asked.

Tom shrugged. 'The house, I guess. Bad shape. But
I never been there. Just heard about it.'

'From who?'

'Truckers. Tourists. There's lots of people up there in
the summer. Folks see the sign, they slow down. Word
gets around.'

'Then there's something wrong with it. Something
else,' Ed had said. And now, driving along strands of
frozen barbed wire that moaned in the wind, the pressure was starting to get to him. Nothing much showed
on his face, but Katherine knew from the way he kept
touching his mustache that he was tired. And cranky.

The wind kicked up dancing devils of icy mist, whirling
dervishes that frittered along the low ridges of snowdrifts
like the squirming panic that had touched her a moment
earlier.

A small, dark dog, some kind of mutt, stepped into
the road ahead, a speck of pepper in a vast salt wasteland.
As they got closer, it grew out of the whiteness like a quick
stain, eyes reflecting the headlights for just a moment,
before slipping across and disappearing into the snow.

Ed said, 'Hell of day for a dog to be out.' Katherine
didn't say anything. She wasn't in the mood to talk. It
had been a long drive for both of them, full of reassur-
ances and attempts at being overly nice one moment,

then harsh, bitter words strung together in half formed sentences the next.

The house loomed into view through the grey, blowing snow, next to a large tree in the center of the driveway. Three barns waited in the fog off to the left. Wind swirled around the dark, yawning doors, big enough to swallow harvesters. A fat orange cat wound its way out of one of the buildings, settled itself back on its haunches and blinked at them.

Ed parked under the tree. Katherine looked out at the property and the chill wriggled all the way down her back this time, and she told herself, quite firmly, to just stop it. These panic attacks or whatever the heck they were - she stopped unbuckling her seatbelt for a moment and wondered if maybe, just maybe, there was a chance she was pregnant. Maybe that was what was making her mind jump at shadows. They'd quit using condoms two months ago. Ed had wanted to calculate her ovulation date, take her temperature, and was going about the whole thing terribly businesslike, but she told him to knock it off. Took all the fun out of it.

If it was true, if she was pregnant, then she'd gladly put up with any sudden panic attacks.

Katherine drew her coat tight and opened her door. The cold hit her like a chainsaw in the chest. For a moment, she couldn't draw a breath. The door shut with a slight chunk and she flinched as the tree above her shivered into colourful movement.

The branches were alive in a bright, flapping blanket. Hundreds of birds flitted about in the dying light; many different sizes, shapes, colours, and species made up the flock. Katherine thought she recognised parrots, parakeets, even a toucan. Then she realised the birds were totally silent. No cries, no calls, no whistling, nothing.

Snow appeared, seemingly growing out of the thin, sharp air, and the entire flock lifted en masse and dissolved like Technicolor static into the clouds.

She turned to her husband, but he was already halfway across the driveway. The wire gate hung open, half-buried in fresh snow. A narrow ditch had been shovelled between two grey pine trees and along the concrete walkway that ran parallel to the house to the back door. She stepped between the trees and got her first good look at the house. Pregnant or not, she hated it immediately.

It erupted out of the ground like a neglected monument, the colour of an old tooth. The sides of the house were streaked with dark stains from rain, like weeping sores that ran down the walls. A candle flickered in the back window.

Katherine felt suddenly nauseous and wondered if it might be morning sickness, even though it was four o'clock in the afternoon. Nothing moved in the house. She bent over and began to retie her boot. She didn't care about the price. She could never see herself living somewhere like this. It wasn't that she was being a snob or anything; she had been fine with several houses that Ed had driven to all over Indiana and even a few in Illinois. Of course, they couldn't afford those; not without her father's help anyways. But this, this place was out of the question.

Ed saw his wife and went back, knelt down with her. 'Listen, I know you and I know what you're thinking. So listen to me. Listen, okay? Anything bad in the house I can fix, okay? I can make it a real home, okay? You'll never have to live in it until you're fine with it. Okay? The house we can fix.' He pointed at the barns. 'I'm thinking about the out buildings. If they're in good shape, and this place is going for the price Tom said, then it'll be worth it.'

He leaned in close. 'Tell you what, show some patience with this place, and I won't drive home tonight. We'll stay at that motel back at the freeway. Eat someplace nice. And have some fun back in the room. Fair enough?'

Katherine squeezed his fingers. 'I'll go in there, but on one condition.'

Ed was silent.

'That I can ask you to leave at any moment. I'm tired, I'm hungry, and I don't feel well. You're right. I don't like this place one bit. But I'll go in there for you. But you have to promise me that you'll leave if I ask.' She knew that she wouldn't have to ask again, that Ed had got the hint that she wanted to leave as soon as possible.

Of course, he hadn't. He nodded and kissed her forehead. 'I promise.' He pulled her up.

Ed went up the concrete steps and knocked briskly at the back door. Katherine drew her coat tighter and put on a smile for the owner. Inside the house, nothing happened. Ed knocked again, louder this time.

They heard pinched, hesitant footsteps.

A stick-like figure appeared. Katherine's first thought, oddly, was a memory. She saw it quite clearly, from a book in her high school history class, a picture taken within a concentration camp.

The old woman looked like one of the camp's prisoners as she leaned out into the cold. Lines appeared to have been cut into her face with an axe. 'Help you folks?' She wore makeup that looked like she'd put it on in the dark, really just a slash of lipstick, a clumping explosion of powdered blush on either side of her face, and an unsteady black eyeliner that drifted up to a startlingly bushy eyebrow.

Her eyes were wide, wide open; she rarely blinked, quickly and deliberately when she did, as if she were afraid to leave her eyes closed for any longer than necessary. Her arms were so thin they might break opening the screen door. She wore a bathrobe that looked like it had been used to clean a furnace. Bare, hairy legs ended in cheap pink slippers. The woman's heels were cracked, blackened with frostbite.

Katherine's second coherent thought was that the old woman really had put her makeup on in the dark; the house had no power. Night was creeping across the frozen land; thick shadows pooled in the snow around the house and barns. The darkness inside the house had a solid, physical quality that Katherine could almost reach out and grab.

Ed realised he could see the slackened folds of skin of the old woman's bare belly through the loosely knotted robe and this made him uncomfortable. 'Ah, hi there. My name's Ed. This is my wife Kath. We've come to ask about the For Sale sign up on the front of your property there.'

Katherine was suddenly thankful for her husband as he took charge, shouldering the responsibility of talking directly to this insane woman. She imagined feeling a kick inside her, the feeling of having Ed's baby deep in her soul, and this calmed her, since he was a part of her now, and she decided to trust him with this property. If he said he'd take care of the house, then believing him was the least she could do.

The woman didn't answer for a while. Her eyes shot everywhere. She looked like she wanted to chew her upper lip off but decorum wouldn't allow it so she patted her robe pocket instead, as if she had a tambourine. Finally, she took her restless hand and leaned against the doorframe, trapping it. 'Yeah. This place is for sale. Why don't you folks come in.' She stepped back inside, letting her restless hand loose, gesturing with it.

Ed took Katherine's hand and said, 'We'd love to.'

Without her husband's hand, full of rough calluses and scars, she would have never been able to step into the house. The floor crunched under their feet as a dry, mealy smell hit them. The old woman lifted a beer can with a candle stuck to the top, revealing a narrow path to the kitchen. The back porch was nearly bursting with dry pet food.

Fifty-pound bags of dog food were piled haphazardly to the ceiling. Bags of cat food too, all different brands, as if the old woman had gone around to the grocery stores in the area and just cleaned them all out of their pet food stocks. It looked to be maybe ten, fifteen carloads worth of pet food. Most of the bags had been slashed open, spilling kernels over the floor. This was what crunched under their boots.

Wonderful, Katherine thought. Trust her husband to find a ranch with a clearly insane owner, one of those women who hoarded cats. Just going through the house was going to wreak havoc with Katherine's allergies. She could imagine the rooms; stuffed with newspapers and garbage and cats. Dozens and dozens of cats. Maybe hundreds. But didn't these people live in the cities?

Katherine studied her coat's zipper, let his hand guide her, and didn't say anything. She followed her husband and decided that if he wanted this ranch, then no matter what, this house was coming down and they would simply have to build a new one.

'Looks like your animals'll be taken care of for a long time,' Ed said.

'This? They don't like it,' the old woman said, and opened the back door. 'They won't eat it.' They moved through a dark mudroom and into the narrow kitchen. 'No power,' she explained. 'I had it shut off.' She put the beer can candle on the counter, shoving small plastic bowls aside. Dishes and cups of all shapes and sizes filled the counters; plates, mixing bowls, metal cat bowls, and even coffee mugs, all full of wet, rotten cat food, covered in mold, fungus, and spider webs. More bags of dry food had been piled where a table might have gone. The old woman lit another candle and led them down a hallway into a living room filled with shadows reluctant to leave.

She knelt in front of the hearth, shoved two logs into the fireplace, side by side, added a third across the top, and shoved a fistful of crumpled bark into the gap. She held the candle to the bark, blowing on it occasionally, and finally got it lit.

'How many acres is the place?' Ed asked.

'Three-fifty. This house sits in the middle. Own the land all the way down to the river.'

'How much are you asking?'

'Fourteen hundred an acre.'

Ed stiffened. 'The house, and out buildings, are they included?'

'Of course.' She threw up her arm and made a weak attempt at a sweeping gesture. 'I hate this place. My husband died here. I want nothing to do with it.' In the gathering flames' light, the old woman began to cry.

Ed and Katherine didn't know what to say, where to look. As the fire grew, they got a better look at the room. The hearth was blackened, with ashes everywhere. A stained child's mattress lay in one corner. A single dining room chair sat in front of the picture window. Other than that, the place was empty. Filthy, but empty. Katherine tried to mentally place their couch in this room, probably in the corner where the mattress laid, and their dining room table, a wedding gift from the bride's parents, over where the chair watched the window.

'How many bedrooms in the house here?' Ed asked.

'Three.'

'Bathrooms?'

'One.'

Ed nodded, cracked his knuckles. Finally he said, 'Say,

you mind if I go take a look at your out buildings? I'd like to see 'em before it gets too dark.'

The old woman shrugged. 'Help yourself.'

Ed forced a smile. 'Maybe you gals can take a look upstairs?'

Katherine glared at her husband. But he was already gone, banging through the back door and out into the snow. She turned back to the old woman.

As if she sensed Katherine's gaze, the old woman spoke without looking up from the fireplace. 'You want to see the upstairs?'

Katherine wanted to shake her head, wanted to follow her husband out the door and climb in the Dodge and leave all of this behind, but she heard herself say, 'Um, please, if it isn't too much trouble.'

The old woman led Katherine to a staircase that squealed and creaked as if they were causing it pain. In the flickering candlelight, Katherine could see her boots and the old woman's slippers left very clear marks in dust so fine it might have been talcum powder. Obviously, the old woman hadn't been upstairs in months. Maybe years.

The rooms were typical of Midwestern farmhouses, cramped wooden boxes with one sliver of a window in each. Katherine was surprised to find each one totally empty, nothing at all like the maze of garbage and cats that she had imagined. In fact, she didn't think there were any cats in the house; that familiar tingling in the back of her throat, the thick tears that welled up in her eyes, that feeling of stuffiness in her nose whenever she visited one of her friends that owned cats, all of the usual symptoms were absent.

But then they found one black and white cat grooming itself in the corner of the last room.

The old woman stomped her foot. 'Hush! You ain't supposed to be inside. You know better. Out!' The cat regarded them coolly for several seconds, then went back to rubbing its paw against its skull. The old woman chewed on her lip, then simply closed the door and they went back downstairs without another word. Paw prints now surrounded their footprints in the dust on the stairs.

Outside, night had well and truly fallen, leaving the world in utter darkness.

The old woman reclaimed her spot near the fireplace and watched the flames silently. Katherine studied her zipper, but the candle in the kitchen beckoned, and her curiosity got the better of her. She drifted down the hallway and watched through the kitchen window as the interior light in the Dodge's cab came on, spilling light onto the fresh snow. Ed had opened the door. A moment later, he switched on a flashlight and went back out to the barns. She watched the beam of yellow light sweep across the snow and up into the rafters of the first barn on the right.

For some perverse reason, maybe just to drive home the final rivet in her resolve to demand the house be destroyed and a new one built, probably closer to the highway, she surreptitiously twisted the HOT handle at the sink.

The faucet thumped, and she got the feeling the pipes were twisting in frustration. A goldfish squirmed out of the faucet and fell flopping into the sink. Katherine jerked back. The fish, maybe three inches long, gasped for liquid oxygen.

The old woman popped into the kitchen. 'Whadja' turn it on for?'

More fish spilled into the sink. The old woman pushed past Katherine and twisted the handle off. She squeezed until the tendons in her forearms shook. 'Now you let them in. You let them all in.'

Katherine caught movement out of the corner of her eye.

Another cat was grooming itself in a cabinet, directly across the kitchen. She blinked. Another sat near a vent in the floor. And she suddenly knew, with the cold certainty of someone falling off a bridge, that something was wrong with these cats. Her allergies had not appeared. Her throat was fine, her nose open, eyes clear. Instead, there was just this escalating sense of unease. Everything about this place felt tainted. Poisoned.

Outside, she heard a dog barking.

She went to the window, and saw the flashlight scanning the second barn.

Something scuttled across the kitchen floor, uncomfortably close to her legs. It was too long and thin and snakelike to be a cat...a ferret maybe? It had come from inside one of the lower cabinets, leaving the open door to bump sluggishly against the drawers next to it. Mouldy brochures spilled from the cabinet.

Katherine picked one up and held it to the candle. A photograph of two kittens filled most of the cover; the smaller one was licking the other's face. Their eyes looked too large. Beneath the photo was a question, 'What will happen to them when you are gone?'

She opened the brochure. Dominating the centre of the brochure was a large, colour photo of a huge, green lawn surrounded by clean cages. Dogs frolicked on the grass. Another picture showed a glass walled room; thick, solid tree branches were strewn throughout the room. Sleeping cats were draped all over the limbs. Surrounding these were more pictures of animals. Dogs, cats, birds, lizards, rodents, every kind of pet Katherine could imagine. There was even a large aquarium. Every animal appeared happy, at peace. To her, the place looked like some sort of huge, incredibly lavish animal sanctuary.

The old woman said, 'That place bought this place. Makes sense, I guess. Since neither one of 'em exist exactly.'

'I'm sorry. What?' Katherine dropped the brochure. It had nothing to do with her. It had nothing to do with her husband. Through the window, she spotted the flash-light beam sweeping the ground as it approached the third and last barn. Thank the Lord. They could finally leave.

The dog barked again. Another joined in, and another.

The flashlight whipped around in a jolting circle.

'That place bought this place,' the old woman repeated, then coughed. 'It was all my husband's idea. Take in all those animals when their owners died and promise to look after them and love them until their dying day. Which wasn't long after. He burned 'em all. Soon as they came in. The clients' sons or daughters or lawyers. They'd bring all their pets in the front door, and my husband would drag 'em right out the back door. Haul 'em off to the incinerator. Dropped 'em in when they were still alive. Sometimes up to a hundred a week.' Her voice dropped to a whisper. 'For years.'

'Look, I really don't care. This is your business. I'm just waiting for my husband.' The flashlight had entered the third barn, and Katherine could just barely make it out, flicking this way and that.

'But this is something you need to know.' The old woman held the candle out to the side, stepping uncomfortably close to Katherine, close enough that Katherine could smell the woman's rancid body. 'All I did was answer the phone. That's all. But it was enough. Enough to damn me. And now you're here, looking to buy this place.' The old woman shook her head slowly. 'That's enough. Enough to damn *you*. This place, this land, was bought and paid for by them.' She jerked the candle at the kitchen door.

Seven or eight cats filled the doorway. A few hissed at the old woman. More waited in the darkness of the hall beyond, eyes throwing back the candlelight as glowing green embers. 'They own it now, not me. They're so, so hungry. They just take and take and take and take—'

Katherine cried out 'Shut UP!' and violently zipped up her coat, snatched the candle off the beer can held by the old woman. She cupped the flame close, nearly squeezing it out. 'Now please. You stay here. Just stay in here. Please. We're leaving.'

She glanced out of the window just in time to see Ed's flashlight beam sweep across the barn ceiling, flip over until it was pointing at the other end of the barn, where it trembled for a moment, then went suddenly still.

Katherine's mouth went dry and she couldn't swallow. She turned away from the old woman and felt more cats brush against her shins as she moved to the back door. Light spilled through her fingers and revealed flickering slices of the kitchen. Cats, some rabbits, one or two ferrets, and a couple of tiny, deformed dogs crawled around and over the bowls of rotten food. Some things that looked like hamsters peeked out of drawers.

Katherine slipped on the pet food strewn across the floor and nearly fell. 'Just stay here, damn it all to hell!' she blurted and backed away from the old woman who made no move to follow. Katherine let the screen door bang shut behind her and edged down the frozen steps. She cupped her hands around the candle and carefully shuffled across the vast driveway, towards the unnaturally still light out in the barn.

She passed the Dodge and decided at the last moment to veer her course, kicking through the fresh snow to the pickup. She jerked the driver's door open and hit the horn three times. Then she bent and listened, fighting to quiet her own racing heart and slow her gasping gulps of frigid air. Clouds of her breath collected around her head and rolled back; it felt like tears on her cheeks.

Not a sound. After the blasts of the horn had faded, it was now so quiet she swore she could hear the snow falling, landing in the tree above her, gently pinging into the metal of the still warm hood, the soft, crisp sounds as it landed in the snow around her. There was no wind. The snowflakes fell straight down, undisturbed by so much as an exhale.

She heard a dog barking. It sounded like it was inside the third barn.

She held the candle high for a moment.

And saw the reflections of dozens, maybe even a hundred, pairs of animal eyes.

Katherine dropped the candle in the snow and ran to the third barn. She found the flashlight, lying alone on the gravel. She grabbed it and sent the light flying around the barn, but the place was empty. Her breathing echoed back at her, but that was all.

Her husband had vanished.

She screamed, 'Ed! Ed!' The snow absorbed the cries, and the sounds died instantly. From the corner of her eye, she thought she saw the reflecting eyes of dogs and cats, but whenever she jerked the flashlight to where she had seen the animals, she saw nothing now but icy gravel and snow. It was maddening, so she kept the light perfectly still, aimed at her feet.

She stood there for a long time, pleading, 'Ed. Ed, please. Please answer me. Please Ed. Please.' A stark, naked need for her husband cracked open deep inside her, leaving a gaping chasm. She shrieked and ran into the snow, whipping the flashlight back and forth in a desperate attempt to see Ed. She dashed through the barns, screaming his name, her sobs alternately echoing inside the empty barns and being oddly muted when she ran back into the snow.

Ed was gone.

But always the eyes. They flickered at the edges of her sight like pinpricks in a grainy eight-millimetre film.

He had to be in the house. He had to be. She ran to the back door and charged up the steps, hollering, 'Ed! Ed!' Just before her hand grasped the door handle, she heard a click. The old woman had locked the door.

Katherine slapped the door, shouting, 'Ed! Open this door! Ed!'

Behind her, a dog barked. She whipped around, flashlight skittering across the snow. At the edge of the light, where the darkness took over, hundreds of shining eyes watched back. The eyes, jumping and glowing with the reflection from the flashlight, were lined up around the yard. More eyes continued to appear, stretching back into the darkness of the fields. The hundreds of eyes swelled into thousands.

'Oh my Lord Holy Jesus,' Katherine breathed into the cold air.

As if obeying some silent signal, the mass of animals seeped into the jittery light. Hundreds of dogs. Thousands of cats. The tropical birds were mixed throughout, hopping nimbly between the other animals. They were joined by hamsters, mice, ferrets. Several iguanas crawled sluggishly through the snow, long tongues tasting the ice. A potbelly pig snorted and snuffled as it moved forward.

They came closer. Closer. Until Katherine finally jumped down the steps and ran for the Dodge. She made it as far as the open space of the driveway before they surrounded her and the falling snow swallowed her screams.

Inside, the old woman pulled her robe tighter. When the sun rose in the morning, she would put on her late husband's coat and slide her feet into his boots and go out to the Dodge. She knew there would be more of the paw prints in the snow now. There had been only a dozen or so when her own husband had been taken years ago. She tried not to think about how many more were coming, drawn to the stink of this place. Some days, especially when she saw a new vehicle, lured by the FOR SALE sign, she wished she could just simply die and be done with all of it. But the animals had been creeping into her dreams, snatching tiny bites of her mind and she knew death would be worse. Far worse. And so tomorrow she would drive down through the trees and out to the river and park on the thick ice. No one from town would be out there until spring, and by then the Dodge would be at the bottom with the others.

She shivered and scooted her chair closer to the fire, caught between a fear that clawed at her soul and a sick hope that someone else would come down the driveway. Soon. Because she was responsible for all the animals. They were her pets now.

And they simply had to eat.

A Different Kind of Sunshine

Peter Gutiérrez

There are sounds in the night you learn to ignore. In a big city walk-up, you tune out that slowly ascending creak-and-whine. In the country, it's those dry leaves on the roof, that dog on the other side of the hill. You hear them, but you make them part of another life, not yours. You don't learn this trick, your eyes blink open a thousand times before dawn.

But of course your listening holds fast to other items. The slide and click of a deadbolt. A child's murmur of distress from the other end of the hallway... That hallway that's always so much longer as you grope along it without contact lenses, without light.

Even when dreaming, you're busy sorting the innocent from what's not. Much as we might like to think otherwise, we can't quite escape the world where sound waves travel on air and where people get hurt by things they don't see coming. The world where rules apply.

I have to watch that: saying *we* or *you* when I really mean *me*. When I really mean *I*.

And who I am is someone doggedly unexceptional. Located neither in city nor country, my home is one of those places you pass quickly on the county road, wondering why someone would choose to live on such a busy thoroughfare. Well, yes, vehicles do stream by constantly, but they hardly trespass on the silence - a honking horn or a blaring radio is a pretty rare thing. Instead, there's mostly a gentle *whooooosh* that puts me in mind of surf.

With the interstate only a mile away, there's also the occasional ten-wheeler. I'll track it as I lie awake, know exactly which pothole it's just discovered, which lies still in wait. First I'll hear the rumble in the empty bedroom and then in here if it's heading north. Or, if it's travelling south, it's the other way around: first in here and then there, my hearing in two places at once.

When you're a parent, you adjust to a different order of night sounds. That toddler cries and it's your turn to do something about it, everything else fades fast. You're moving before you're awake – not stumbling, because you've done this too many times to be clumsy – and not turning on the lights – because then everyone would be as irritated as you and the baby.

You don't really have thoughts, but if you did, they'd be very simple. *My child is crying, and it's my job to stop it*. After all, Laurie handled all of those middle-of-the-night feedings during the first few months, didn't she? So what if you go to work every day and she's the one who can schedule an afternoon nap?

There was a time when an entire family called this house home. That family, it used to be mine. Although you can't quite term what I have now a 'family' (it's better than that in a lot of ways), it's not like I'm sitting around pining for a return to the good old days.

And no, as a rule, I don't allow visitors here anymore. They just wouldn't understand.

Anyway, that's how I ended up dealing with the night terrors, the I'm-colds or the whatever-it-is-this-times. It wasn't every night that the monitor jolted me awake, just a couple of times a week - more, obviously, after Abigail was born and there were two kids to listen for. You hear something over the receiver, an indistinct mewling, and at first you don't know who it is. There's a small *oh no oh no*, and you don't know if it's Abigail's chipmunky voice or just her big sister regressing.

In any case, you're on the scene, stroking the hair, lifting the pillow from the floor, fetching the plastic cup of water. You get weekends off for good behaviour. That may seem backwards, but that's the way it is: Laurie's with the kids 'all day' so you sacrifice part of your sleep. That's you being a good dad.

As far as this *you* business is concerned, please don't take it personally. I suppose it's my way of saying that the life I have now could be anyone's life. It's neither punishment nor reward.

What's that Laurie used to say to her friends on the phone? With that tone of resignation passing as maturity?

I remember now. The kind of statement that covers a multitude of sins from a multitude of sinners. There's laziness in it, but it's a wised-up, suburban brand of laziness.

It is what it is.

Sure, some nights I wasn't so quick to respond. I'd lie there and dimly process the sounds from the monitor, both its transmission and my head filled with static. I'd pause on that threshold and strike a deal between me and myself: *if there's one more audible word, just one,* then *I'll go in there.*

I never felt guilty about this because the two sisters, sharing the same room, rarely woke each other. And Laurie was dead to the world with those earplugs in, so I'd lie there, staring at the ceiling through my eyelids.

Waiting for the nameless, momentary anxiety that had broken to the surface to turn and plunge once again into the depths.

My kids never needed a nightlight, never had a fear of the dark. Children, I found to my surprise, can actually learn to like it if you encourage them. 'Darkness is always around you,' my ex would say to our two blond beauties. 'But it can't actually hurt you, ever. Just think of it as just a different kind of sunshine.'

Okay, so maybe that's a little creepy, I thought, but there's no real harm done. It's one of those flavourless, grey market lies that adults constantly feed kids and that kids always forget within a couple of years. Laurie had a backlog of such tidbits of metaphysical 'wisdom.' I don't know where exactly she got that particular line about darkness, but chances are it was something she read or at some meeting or lecture. She was always attending meetings and lectures.

Once I tried to compliment her about this, on how she had so many different interests. She just looked at me, deadpan, and said that she wasn't really interested in gardening and current books and the school system and all the rest of it.

'I go to meetings,' she explained, 'so that someone will listen to me.' I didn't know what to say to this, so I just let it hang there. Then she walked by me and out of the room, and on her way out she said, 'Exactly.'

I don't date, and the few friends I have keep asking why. I can tell that they think it's related to some wound to the psyche or libido that I've suffered. Yet the truth is fairly straightforward: dating would necessitate going out in the evenings, and every night, without exception, I need to be here. There's just no way around that.

Although I didn't have monitor duty every night, that doesn't change that over time I came to be *always* listening. Laurie had deferred her listening to mine so much that I'd be on alert even on nights that weren't mine. I'd be listening right through the earplugs because deep down inside, I didn't know it wasn't my turn.

I suppose I'm trying to explain how I became like this, with my hearing in two places.

It's nice to think that the root cause was my being so vigilant. So concerned with my kids' welfare and all that, working by day to provide for them and doing guard duty by night. A large, shadowy benefactor who'd swoop in to provide all manner of comfort and protection to those who'd strayed into the realms of nightmares or wet beds.

The truth is, I didn't think about my kids much, not consciously, not actively. Certainly I loved them. I'm not trying to make myself the bad guy here. In fact, maybe it's *because* I loved them (cowardly self-justification rarely begins any other way, I know) that I hardly gave them thought. I couldn't bear the idea of a future where they'd no longer be so precious, where I'd no longer be so adored.

Logically speaking, when Abby turned three, maybe earlier, we should have got rid of the monitor. Told her to get out of bed and come get us if there was a problem. But we babied her a bit. Plus, as Laurie pointed out, having a 'spy' in their room allowed us to hear whether the two of them were actually sleeping or just yammering from bed to bed, giggles and whispers blending into a language that brought a smile to my face despite the defiance it signified.

When we lost Abigail, I didn't use those types of memories as touchstones, much to my surprise. I don't know whether this was obvious to Laurie and others, but I don't see how it could have been. They're my thoughts after all. How can you look at a person and tell how deeply they're grieving? You'll always give them the benefit of the doubt, assume that they're consumed.

That's what I count on these days, actually: for folks to think the best of me by thinking the worst of my experience, by imagining extremes of deprivation that simply don't exist.

Alison figured out that I usually got the same bus from the city, that its arrival time was more or less reliable, so she and Abby began timing my five-minute walk from the bus stop. I'd stroll down the street, a bounce in my step for the first time that day, see our bright yellow frame house, and there in the picture window, two angels bouncing up and down on the sofa, waving to me frantically, shouting and sending me kisses, silent on the other side of glass. The last eleven hours of commuting and office drudgery would melt away and I'd get an ache: *why can't this moment – this one right here – why can't it be the one that's half a day long?*

I'm not sure why I'm recounting this. Was it to support some point? Show the kind of emotional touchstones I just finished saying that I did without...?

It's okay, though. I'm all right. Not that that's always been the case. But these days if I'm confident about anything, it's that I have the life that suits me best.

Was I better off a couple of years ago? Yes, but I guess that's where *it is what it is* comes in: an acceptance both that things are rarely as good as they once were, but also seldom as awful as we'd imagined they would be.

People always talk about how their lives changed, how they became 'different' people, their biographies neatly partitioned, after having children. The truth is, it's nothing compared to the break after a child is gone. If this seems overly dramatic, think about it. You spend your young adulthood, maybe your childhood, imagining being a parent – you can't help it to a degree. But how much time is given to contemplating the subtraction of all that?

Laurie and I reacted to Abby's death the same way

we had to a million other incidents in our marriage: we looked around for someone to blame. I swore I hadn't heard any distress that night – not a thing. I wanted to say, 'It probably wouldn't have mattered anyway, given how fast they say she went,' but offering that kind of observation would have smacked of defensiveness. As if claiming, *I didn't hear anything and even if I did...*

The doctors, if they'd been asked explicitly, would have confirmed that Abby hadn't cried out. Then again, these were the same doctors who said that short of regular cardio exams, there was no way to have predicted what happened. That is, no way to know that the 'innocent' heart murmur which had been diagnosed at birth had suddenly grown up. Abby's paediatrician never said, 'Oh, you better run those tests again – after almost four years, she's due for an update.' No, nothing like that. The attitude was more like, 'Yep, there it is again. That murmur.'

Have you ever really looked at a stethoscope? How it splits the doctor's hearing down two long tubes and then rejoins it at the point where the lungs and heart and gut are listened to? The patient is told how to breathe and the doctor listens right into those breaths, at all those internal squalls and quakes and potholes that otherwise can't be detected.

It's funny that now I can't much recall the words Abby said during the time she spent with us. Well, I can recall the *words*, but not the sound of her saying them.

What stays with me, though, what's never left: the night-time coughs and sneezes, the gentle snores backed by the stroke of the furnace cycling on, the sharpened scuttle of squirrels chasing each other from branch to gutter and back again.

I didn't mean to suggest, earlier, that Laurie ever came out and accused me of negligence. Instead, she was probably unable to separate these specific events from the general failure that was our life together.

Never gave much thought to Laurie's own memories of Abby, to what policy she had developed toward them. Maybe she'd stare at the floor and recall the way her child's bare feet looked. Or glance in the rearview while driving and see, for a second, Abby asleep in her car seat. I don't know because she never talked about it. At least not with me.

One thing I'm certain she sees – the salty crusts, so small, where Abby's final tears had squeezed out and dried upon her face.

But I saw something else there: calm. As if the tears had dried long before she passed.

There's nothing to do when a child is dead in front of you. It's different, has to be, if she's dying and you're in her presence. But when it's done and over, there's nothing to think about: your body tells you what to do. You make noises and gestures, you grab things and each other. You make phone calls. Then others are there, the ones accustomed to dealing with death, and you take your cues from them.

Later, when the officials and doctors and documents have left you alone and your mind is yours once again, it doesn't quite know what to do. Conscious choice has been out of the picture for too long. The conventional emotions you feel day to day – being pissed off, amused, vaguely anxious, aroused – all of these return as if from a long journey, one that's left them old and tired.

It was my job to put Abby's stuff in storage. But when I came across the monitor, I couldn't bear to part with it. I suppose it represented solid evidence of having been a father to a person who no longer existed.

Abby was always clingy. Apparently she'd make a game of it at the mornings-only preschool she attended, not letting go when she saw how easily her mother was stopped by others' scrutiny. Later, Laurie would scold but not punish her; she couldn't bring herself to be too harsh to a child whose only crime was to hug her leg, even if such affection was largely a sham.

That first time I turned the monitor on again was also the first time I'd wept since the funeral – when the weeping was primarily in reaction to what I saw in the faces of Abby's grandparents.

When I switched on the receiver in my room, it was probably out of self-punishment or maudlin nostalgia. Definitely not a sense of discovery or hope.

At first I heard wind mixed with silence, then something that sounded like branches hitting the windows, and then, as I've described, cars arriving a few seconds before they reached me.

At first.

The way Laurie and I squared our accounts: she has Alison, I have the house. Since this town is still a good commute for me, this arrangement makes sense.

I see Alison, of course, but never at the bright yellow house, and I'm not sure if that makes sense to her or if it hurts her feelings. To be honest, I'm not a very good father to her. If she only understood, though, how much more Abby needs me. How otherwise she's all alone.

Alison and I don't talk about her much, and when we do, it's like we're discussing a friend who moved across the country. Alison's a strong girl, which you wouldn't predict if you knew her parents. It must have helped that she was spared seeing her sister that morning. Always the early riser, Alison had simply left the bedroom first, believing Abby still asleep.

Now, when I hear the small, static-filled voice call in the night, I don't get up. Instead, I reply as soothingly as I can, my voice travelling through the house – I'm not as quiet as I used to be since there's no one to wake up anymore. Now I answer immediately instead of hoping the sound will go away and let me sleep.

Shhh, it's all right, I'll say. *Daddy's here. Don't be afraid of where you are. I know it's dark there, but remember what Mommy used to say...*

I wait, hoping that does the trick. That then I'll hear *good night, daddy* and the sound of those two lips blowing me a kiss down that long, long hallway that separates us.

People sometimes ask, trying to sound casual, 'You still in that house?'

There's a question behind that question of course. They want to know how I manage to stay on here, the past being what it is. Or how I can bear to be alone.

I let them think those thoughts, but then I see the sadness in their eyes and I smile. 'It's not so bad,' I say, shrugging. 'It is what it is.'

Swept Away

Samuel Minier

Mary returned from Niagara, if she ever really did, with two suitcases and no child. After the police had questioned her, consoled her, released her, she returned to the hotel and gathered everything – his toys and clothes and shoes, her souvenir shirt, their ticket stubs from the black-light mini-golf, that STUPID, HORRIBLE headless Chippewa Chief pencil he'd begged for. She wedged it all in their suitcases, lugged them back to the same observation deck, and then strew into the Horseshoe, jumping up and down while doing so, screaming, his suitcase lid banging, gulping, gaping like a mouth vomiting out the detritus of their vacation.

The Falls flushed it all away as easily as they had her son.

The police returned, of course. They recognised her, of course. They feared what she might throw in next, so a female officer a few years Mary's senior played like a mother, an arm around and a voice low, while another voice re-verified via mobile phone that yes, someone was coming, they were an hour out of Buffalo now, and so the police held her, the officer-mother quite literally, until the family arrived with brakes like screeches and sobs to match. They loaded Mary and the two suitcases into one car, and some other relative got into Mary's own car, and then the two cars crossed over Rainbow Bridge, heading home.

And as Mary re-entered the States, she looked down into the Falls for their...well, his...his debris. Which of course was ridiculous, the possessions being hours drowned and anyway, it was night. But both American and Canadian Falls were lit up, foam like fluorescent cotton candy, and Mary could easily see all of it bobbing down there – the pencil, whose Indian-headed eraser he had ripped off and thrown into the river seconds before his own plunge; the ticket stubs, glowing fish remembering a golf game that ended in a temper tantrum and a broken windmill on Hole 16; the 'I Heart Niagara' shirt, in her favourite baby blue, with a not-small stain from a thrown meat ball intended for her face; his toys, clothes, shoes, everything of him that had somehow soured in one blinding, blistering second. A curdling of love.

Yes, in the turbulent Easter froth Mary could see what no one else could, or had – her hand, not grasping for him as he stood atop the rail. Yes, the hand was in motion, but no, no, oh god that wasn't a grasp.

Septophobia

Simon Nightingale

The ad said it was a comfortable, self-contained bedsit. Single bed, kettle, desk and chair. It's a fucking hole, that's what it is. Damp, cold, small. Noisy. First on the left, straight after the front door. Furthest from the dungeon they call a kitchen; furthest from the bathroom. Nearest to the street; nearest to the fucking phone. I hate that phone. Ring-ring-fucking-ring, all day long. The others know I hate it. That's why they never answer it. It's probably them that get people to phone. Just to piss me off. Fuckers! And I can't not answer it. The ringing just gets to me. Four squeals and it's in my head. 'Answer me, answer me, answer me...'

'Is Andy there?'

'What the fuck do you think? Has he ever answered when you've rung before?'

'Room four, please.'

'Yeah. Right. Like I'm the fucking switchboard operator!'

And it knows when I'm in. Which is nearly all the time, I admit. But never once while I was out did they

71

leave a message on the pad by the phone. Not once. Not that I expect to find messages for me. I don't really know anybody. If I did, nobody would ring me anyway. Never been one for talking. Especially on the phone. But no messages at all? Not even for the others? No, they've been planning. But I know. I'm on to them.

So I've worked it all out. You see, it's all about numbers. They're fucking everywhere, man. Hiding behind your names. Lost in petals and leaves. Shapes. Distances. Clocks. Everything is just one big number code. And they rule you, these numbers. You'd be different if you hadn't been tenth on the register at school, if you hadn't had to get the number nine bus to work. Even your fucking TV is just numbers floating through the air, rearranged on the screen, the odd wave messing with your brain. Everything is numbers in the end. That's why there's seven fucking rooms in this house. Seven! The last digit of our phone number. The month I was born in. The number of times I've attempted suicide. Fuck! Seven scares the shit out of me. And next week it'll be seven months that I've been in this fucking hole. So I've been looking at the numbers. And now I know what I've got to do. You see, you can change numbers. Even phone numbers; but that won't stop the fucker ringing all day. Simple really. Like at school. Adding and taking away. In my case it'll be taking away. Too many sevens.

I've done all the maths. Maths was always my favourite at school. That and chemistry, which was mostly maths really. Anyway, someone has to go. Shame, though; I'd have liked to have added someone. But the rooms are too small to double up in and it'd be one more person for the phone to ring for. So I've been opening their mail, see which of the bastards are sevens. I know their names now. Tracey has to go. Tracey Black. Jesus, it's obvious. You see, each letter is a number. A is one, B is two. All the way through to Z, which is twenty-six. Now, you have to break these bigger numbers down. Take the letter P. P is sixteen. But you can't have more than one digit. The real number is still hiding. So you add them together. One plus six. P is just as bad as seven. Fuck, it *is* seven. Yeah, I know its only her surname that is seven. But they were clever. *Black*. You know. Magic. Witches. That was obvious, I suppose. How could you miss it? No, the real clever thing is the whole name. Tracey Black. Nine plus seven. Sixteen. One plus six. Seven, just like P. I knew there was something about that P. P. As in 'Phone'.

But when they're that smart you've got to be careful. I mean, really careful. They know more about numbers than anyone. Of course they fucking do, the evil bastards. How else would they have come to be sevens? So I watched. Waited. Worked things out. But you can't just go taking numbers away like that, whenever you feel like it. Changing the numbers is well risky. You've got to be sure. Dead sure. Well, I *am* sure.

And it's the fucking phone that convinced me. The number is 142857, less all the dialling codes. They don't count because they're not specific to our house. I didn't see it at first. Last number's seven, I know, but add them up and you get twenty-seven. Add those two digits

together and it's nine. That stumped me. *Nine*? But then
I remembered. There's not just adding and taking away.
You can times and divide numbers. So I scribbled away.
142857 times two gives you 285714. Times it by three
and you get 428571. Times four: 571428. See? The same
fucking numbers. Repeated like a prophecy. Even the
order of the numbers is the same. That just blew me
away. Until I got to seven. 142857 times seven changes.
Our phone number times by the number of people in
our house gives you 999999. Two emergency numbers
calling me. Two upside down 666s warning me.

I'll have to act soon, though. Restore the harmony.
Then we'll all be happier and maybe the phone will stop
ringing so much. I've got it all worked out. Timing is
going to be important. I've got to avoid sevens, of course.
But that won't be too difficult. Just got to work out when
is the best time. It's the how that's going to be risky. See,
I'll have to get her on her own. Just the two of us. Shit!
that scares me. What if she knows I'm on to her? What
if the others are in on it as well? But I know she likes
girls. I've been spying on her. Skinny girls. Small breasts,
short hair. Like me. Though I doubt they have the same
scars on their arms as I do. Still, it's pretty clever.
Listen:

'Hi, Trace!'

'Oh, err, hi...'

'I know we've never spoken or anything, but...' – I'll
smile a lot. Less than seven seconds at a time, but I'll
smile some – '...I'm Sarah. Listen. I've got a few phone
messages for you. And like, well, a bottle of wine. South

African. It's good stuff. We should get to know each other, like, you know, living in the same place and all.' And then she'll smile. Hopefully think I'm hitting on her.

'Err... Yeah – '

'I've made us something to eat. Wasn't sure if you're a veggie. So I did veggies. Everybody eats vegetables. It's OK, they're organic. With couscous. Any time after seven. OK?'

I know I'm good at persuading people. Mixture of insistent pleading and expectant puppy dog eyes. Being provocative helps too. Anyway, you get the idea. It's not as if she's just going to agree to it right away. I know I'll have to be at my best to persuade her. And I can be sexy if I have to. I've only done it three times, twice with other girls and once with a load of people. But they all did what I wanted. Exactly what I wanted. Which wasn't the sex. That's disgusting. No, it was just to see if I could get them to do things. Man, you'd be amazed at what you can get people to do. Just a nice trimmed pussy and some promises and they're all yours. Anyway, she'll arrive after seven. That's important. Don't want her in my room when the clock strikes seven – no fucking way.

'Hi, Trace, come in,' I'll say.

'Thanks. I brought this bottle of wine.' Or whatever; could be beer. Or whisky. Whatever. It will help though. They've always been easier when they've had a bit to drink.

'It's nearly ready. I've just got to warm the couscous in the microwave. Here. Have a glass of wine.'

'Thanks, Sarah. Cheers.' She'll smile. I'll smile back.

'Oh, yeah! Here's the messages. All girls. This one – Mandy – seemed especially desperate to get in touch.' And then we'll get personal over the meal. And when she's had enough to drink she'll not even know what hit her. If she's up for a bit of bondage, she'll not even make a noise. And if she's not, I can always persuade her.

And then I'll have to get rid of the body. Well, the number seven. It's not the body. That's only what we see. It's the number that's important, the number that needs to be taken away. Subtracted. Did you know that five is just as strong as two sevens? Yeah. Fourteen is the same as two sevens, no? Add the digits together: one plus four. That's five. And I'm a five, you see. Sarah Deans. That's me. A two plus three. A five. Just like sulphuric acid. H2SO4. Remember your chemistry at school? Work it out! It's a five. Of course, I'll have to cut her into small bits first. Five will be too big, so I thought seven would be nice. Ironic and all. Seven dissolving in five. But maybe I'd better do the maths. Better to be sure – dead sure – when you're dealing with sevens.

Shuck

Rebecca Lloyd

Thrubend Edge is a backwater settlement all boldly laid out on a forgotten road through an agricultural landscape with few trees. It has a look about it that suggests it came together by happenstance and yet has been there forever. It has a church whose grimy steeple pokes rudely upwards at the sky, a tiny store and a derelict scout hut, and a single row of redbrick council houses all grim-faced against the wind that growls across the landscape the whole time.

Liz's house is close to an abandoned chicken farm overlooking a vast chalky field with a wide drainage ditch in front of it. I wondered if it was sheer perversity that made her decide to move there; a way of saying that living alone is such an unnatural thing to do that the place she tried it in must be truly abject. She'd made the decision in one of her rational phases, having accepted reluctantly that life was not a lesser thing without a lover.

The walk from the station was a lengthy one, and I wished I'd started the journey earlier for the night was rotten black, and had me so nervous that I became convinced I'd never get there at all. I started back twice, as if my intention to reach the house had been overruled by some deeper half-formed knowledge, but I forced myself to turn about and face the long dark way again. I was aware all the time of the slimy drainage ditch on my right and kept to the far verge away from it. The field beyond was newly ploughed and the soil, heavily furrowed, was a-glint with white chalk.

'The road's *much* longer at night,' Liz said, as she pulled me inside. 'You should've come at a decent time. I made mince with carrot pieces for lunch and now it's cold. Nobody goes up and down that road at night, anyway.'

'Well, thanks for leaving the door open for me. You didn't have to.'

'It's been open all day; we've been waiting.'

'Is it a Roman road? It never seemed to end.'

'Much older, apparently. It's called The Way. One of those tracks humans made at the beginning of time. You look awful. You haven't even asked me if I'm all right.'

'Are you all right, Liz?'

'More or less, since you ask.'

I tried to shake off the last flitting remnants of fear that had been so powerfully with me outside. 'It's horribly remote here.'

'Oh, to you it would seem like that; you have to be

a certain kind of person to really appreciate the subtlety of it.'

For the first couple of days, I thought about nothing but the nastiness of Liz's house with its flimsy doors and vicious drafts. The wallpaper had patterns of cornucopias that stuck out from its surface in silver swirling ridges. The same wallpaper was in all the rooms including the poky kitchen.

I checked the fridge, she had plenty of food, and Mother was sending her money regularly, so I tried to dismiss my sense that things were not right with her at all. It was September, and cold, but she never closed the front door. Then I began to notice a deep and unusual watchfulness in her; I'd come across her staring through the front window at the field's horizon as if in a trance, and there was something about the rigidity of her posture that made me know she lingered there for hours.

'What're you thinking about, Liz?'

'I'm waiting. I want you to see something. Watch with me.'

The clouds were massing with horrible intensity and a promise of deadly cold rain, and the great undulating field was dotted with rooks. 'Are you really OK here?' I asked, and pushed her hair back over her shoulder. She shuddered almost imperceptibly, but I felt it. 'You're looking restless.'

'I'm fine; I haven't had any episodes for a long time now, unless this new way of thinking is part of it all. That's why I asked you to come.'

'New way of thinking?'

'It's to do with him. I see what I see about him, yet I know something else, and the something else doesn't belong in ordinary life.'

I stepped back so she couldn't see my face. She didn't turn around. 'Who are you talking about?' I could hear her breathing. She wasn't going to say anything else unless I prized it out of her, and I'd long since given up playing that particular game with Liz. 'I'm going to walk around outside a bit. Are you coming?' I looked for signs of another person as I went, an extra coat on the door, a man's boots, but saw nothing but the pointless knick-knacks my sister took with her everywhere like talismans.

She joined me at the gate and waited for me to question her, moving a stone about with her foot. 'Has Mum been up here?' I asked.

'No. It's too far. Anyway, I don't want her to; I just want to show you something.'

'Well, here I am.'

'I'm not alone, you know. You might think I am, but I'm not.'

'I thought that's what you came to Norfolk for, so when you got old, you'd be all practised at not being dependent on somebody else.'

She laughed. 'Well, there's alone and alone.'

The rooks rose suddenly, making no noise as they moved towards the single tree on the field's horizon. 'What do you mean?'

'Well, when he does come, it's as if he's just making

sure I'm still here, and when he's not here anymore it takes me a long time to realise it.'

'Do you want my frank opinion? This is a rotten place you've come to. I think you should come home.'

'I knew you'd say that.'

'We've been through things like this before.'

'No we haven't, Erica. This is different.'

'OK. What's his name?'

'I call him Fin.' I turned to look at her for signs of agitation. Her face was flushed and her hair hung long and glorious.

'Where did you find him, barn dance or something?'

'He came across that field.'

'And you looked at each other and it was true love, again?'

'In a manner of speaking.'

'What were you doing in the field?'

'I was here, by the gate. I thought he'd come out of the ditch, but I mustn't have been looking.'

'So when do I meet him?'

'Tomorrow maybe. I need you to help me. I want to know where he goes.'

'Ask him.'

She shook her head. 'I don't want to say anything else right now; you'll see when you see.'

'It sounds like one of your obsessions.'

'Possession more like, I'm bound to him.'

'Liz, I'm not going to lecture you, because you've heard it all before.'

'What he does isn't right; I want you to witness it.'

'Fin's not why you came here. You've got to stick to your purpose.'

She sighed and turned back to the house. I followed her. 'He's not really a man,' she said quite suddenly and stopping on the path. 'Only he doesn't seem to be what he should be either. I don't want to say anything else in case it blurs your idea of him.'

'When do I meet the boy?'

'He comes in at any old time, there's no rhyme or reason to it. He's a dog, Erica. Well, that's not right, he isn't really.'

'For Christ's Sake, Liz, are you saying he treats you badly?'

'Not exactly; sometimes I feel so safe that I know it's unnatural, then other times I feel singled out and it's horrible. I can't describe it and I can't do anything about it.'

Fin came in the late afternoon just before dark. I wasn't aware of him at first, yet the front room was tiny. Liz took my face in her hands and turned it in the right direction as if I was a kid. 'There, just inside the door.'

'Where?'

'Don't be silly Erica, just inside the door on the right.'

I did see him then. I remember a brutal surge of repulsion welling up in me, and Liz tugging at my arm.

'You can see him, can't you?' she whispered. 'Don't stare Erica, please.'

'Where did he come from?' He was huge and muscled, and crouching. Everything about the house seemed different in his presence, drawn inwards, suffocating.

'I told you. I didn't want to say much, I wanted to know the way you saw him.'

'How do you see him?'

'Unearthly,' she whispered. 'I want to know where he goes. Can you find out?'

'Hell, no.' I pulled her backwards into the kitchen and shut the door between him and us.

'Please, Erica.'

'I think you should leave here. Come back with me tomorrow.'

'No. All I need you to find out is if he's mine or not. Because I am surely his.'

I thought of the time Liz was convinced that people could get through a crack in her windowpane and how she kept a spoon under her mattress to fight them in case they came in at night. I'd grown used to that kind of thing, but now, for the first time, I felt truly terrified of being her twin. I thought a portal had opened up between us that I'd accidentally blundered through into the mire of her fractured mind. Yet, as each of us stared at the other – into our own face – my journey along The Way seemed, in its sudden assault on my memory, to have distinctly heralded the coming of Fin.

The store at Thrubend Edge was in the front room of the last house in the terrace, it doubled as a post office. I was shocked at how quickly the woman there responded to me. It was as if she already knew what I'd come for. 'The black one, I reckon you mean,' she murmured, and with a sort of country rudeness gazed at me from head to foot. 'Try the Warden; he'll be around the church now.' She turned her back on me so abruptly that I gasped and stood for a moment motionless.

I ran through the same cyclical thoughts about my sister that had been with me for years as I made my way towards the church, and felt the familiar old anger all bound about with pity that I could never quite rid myself of. I decided I'd leave Thrubend Edge the following day and never return; Mother would have to deal with Liz by herself. The yew tree at the lychgate had shed its load, and there were thousands of fleshy cup-like berries scattered on the path, some crushed and slimy, and those freshly fallen had a black seed, like a tongue, poking repulsively from their ends. I avoided them and made my way between the gravestones. I'd tell Liz some work had come up, and that I had to get back fast.

It was as if the Warden had seen me coming; he stepped out in front of me from behind a monstrous slanting tombstone waving his arms in the air. 'I'm surprised you dare to come here,' he said.

'The woman at the post office said I should.'

'If that's true, she was mistaken to do so.' He looked

sideways without moving his head as if checking the gravestones for signs of vandalism. 'I'll talk to her. Go away.'

'I wanted to ask you something. I'm staying at the house that stands by itself back along The Way.'

'I know where you live. Leave now, please!' He looked upwards at the bank of cloud that had gathered slowly into a heavy brown mass above us. 'You should never have come to Thrubend in the first place.'

I watched his confusion for a moment. 'I'm Elizabeth Copeland's sister.'

He glanced over his shoulder at the church door and bit his lip. 'I thought you were her.'

'You know my sister, then?'

'Everybody knows her,' he said, and left an idea hanging between us that alarmed me.

'Has she done something strange?'

He shrugged. 'It's not her fault she's chosen, I suppose. Leastways you can't tell if there's something about a person that makes it so. Could be any one of us.'

'Yes, you're right, but chosen isn't the word I'd use to describe it – it's kind of you, though.'

'She might be all right.'

'She says she's all right.'

'I mean her not being from here might make her safe. I know what you've come for, you see.'

I sensed that he did, and the trickling of fear I'd felt

in the post office gathered strength. 'In that case, have you seen him around here?'

'Not yet. I'll have that pleasure before the day is through though.'

'He hangs about in Liz's house, and then suddenly goes.'

The Warden shifted and looked at his watch. 'I can't talk to you outside now.'

I stared at him hard. 'You implied that some people aren't safe here.'

'Nobody ever knows who he'll harm and who he won't.' He laughed suddenly, and peered at me. 'You don't really see him properly, do you; am I right?'

'Yeah, I do. He's huge, black and beautiful.'

'The real blackness is in his soul.' He stared about him once more as if to catch something out not quite hidden from view. 'How is your sister, really, in your opinion?'

'In love.'

'I'd call it enchantment. There's always one.'

'Where does he come from?'

'Hell,' the Warden replied under his breath.

'I'm being perfectly serious.'

'And I'm being perfectly serious. Persuade her to leave with you.'

'So you *do* think he'll harm her?'

'It depends. Look, come with me now, there's a particular window I watch from.'

We stood beside each other and stared through one of the tiny diamond-shaped panes. We had a clear view of the graveyard, and as we waited, I could smell the Warden's fear, like a mingling of rust and fungus, half-chemical and half-organic.

Fin came into sight from nowhere, and I felt something sour fill my mouth and bolt back quickly, leaving it dry as bone. And there, in the silence of the church, I began to acknowledge what I had refused to see before. Even as he drifted, perversely imprinted on the scene, I clung to blatant denial – but as the last remnant of doubt slid out of reach, and I could entice nothing back in support of the rational, I was left with a brutal knowingness of what I was witness to; something occult and degenerate, occult and intimate with my twin.

His presence warped the surroundings so things solid faded and skewed. Behind his body, I was aware of the trunks of spindly trees, yet his movements bore no natural relationship to them. He seemed at times to exist in mid air, and at other times to be made of the very earth itself. He lingered, and turned his head in our direction one more time than seemed coincidental. The Warden shifted back a step or two, and I heard him hiss, 'Move away, he knows you're here.'

The hound was gone suddenly, and where he'd been turned to innocent space and light, but I gazed fixedly at it for a long time, as if it could only be a moment before the scene was flooded again with the flat greyish half-light he'd brought with him. When I finally turned round, I saw the Warden hunched in the front pew. I moved towards him, and could not hear the sound of my own feet; I was walking erratically and stopping sometimes. I noticed that the face of the wooden Christ on the altar was desperate, not with sorrowful agony, but primitive terror.

I slid into the pew directly behind the Warden and stared at the back of his bent neck. 'The Vicar?' is all I could find to say.

'Taken. They all are. The last was here less than five months. He threw himself into the ditch, singing like an idiot as he drowned himself.'

'Liz waits for it. She lingers,' I whispered.

'People say it hunts for soul mates. Since your sister's been here, there've been more sightings. Where I come from he's Padfoot, I never did encounter him there all through my childhood; here they call him Shuck. He waits at the crossroads, or comes suddenly out of the ditch. He runs in Farrow's Field close to the house Miss Copeland's in.'

He turned around and looked all over my face as if it was strange territory, and I knew that having shared the sighting together meant I would remember his face in every detail, that I'd been drawn into a hideous mental intimacy with him against my will. 'It does not exist,' he said.

'It does not exist,' I whispered back.

She was standing as I'd left her, at the window in the front room. 'Did you find out?' she asked, without turning round.

I was glad she couldn't see my face, for I knew it'd stiffened. 'Nobody in the village has ever heard of him,' I said.

'That's of no significance,' she answered, and shifted from foot to foot. 'You didn't see him, then?'

My journey back to the house had been so clouded with fear that I could scarcely remember the walk. 'No. I never saw him.' I stared at her back, willing her to believe she had created him herself.

'Where did you go to look?'

I'd heard the heavy, labouring beat of my own heart all the way through the village and down The Way, and the sound of it increased my terror, for I needed all my senses clear if he were to manifest before me from the ditch, the hedgerow, the very earth itself. I ran, half doubled over, aware that I was whining and sobbing in turn. 'Where do you think I should've gone, Liz?'

'To the churchyard,' she whispered.

'I did. I waited there a long time.'

'I don't believe you.'

Every second I'd expected the apparition to halt me on the road. I sensed it'd been aware of my presence in the church. 'I met the Warden there; he said there is no dog like that.'

Liz turned round slowly. I couldn't see her face properly against the yellowing light from the window. 'You saw him yourself, here,' she answered simply.

As I reached the house and stopped for a second to calm myself, the rooks in the field rose as a single entity, soundless, and headed for the tree on the horizon. 'I saw what you saw, Liz, and that's because I love you, and miss you. Why don't you come home with me?' She shuffled towards me then, and as she put her arms around me, I was both repelled and glad. 'Why don't you get dressed properly, and we'll go home. You've only got one sock on.'

'You did see him when he came here, didn't you?'

'I saw what was in your mind's eye.'

'It's because we're the same people,' she whispered. 'Sometimes I hate you because of it, and sometimes I know really that I am you, and that's why I keep thinking things will be all right in the end. Because you cope with everything, Erica, I mean. So I can in the end.'

'Come back with me.' Even as I said it, I knew she'd refuse. 'The dog isn't real, you know.'

I left the next morning, very early. Liz was already up, she'd torn the wallpaper off around the frame of the window; ragged pieces of it lay curled at her feet. She didn't say goodbye.

I can't keep the ordinariness of things around me anymore. I feel as if there's nothing much solid about the physical world, and nothing innocent, as if what separates things normal from those occult is so flimsy that at any moment terrifying change could occur. I see the Warden at the oddest times; the image of his face is lodged behind my eyes, and it comes to me repeatedly and suddenly. He mouths the words, 'The thing does not exist,' and I repeat it like a child. I am trapped in a hideous limbo in which I both accept and deny the thing.

I've been back to Thrubend Edge once or twice, but cannot get Liz to leave the place. I take supplies down there and clean her house up, but I won't stay overnight. The garden's gone to coarse tangles and rampant grass grows everywhere about. She wanders up and down The Way and across the chalky field in her tattered bathrobe, calling the black dog incessantly. She blames me for its disappearance and thinks that if I'd never shown up in the first place, he'd be with her still. She believes I've always taken her luck away. 'You disturbed something,' she says, 'something vital and urgent. But you wait, you're my twin, if he doesn't come back to me, he'll find you someday, Erica, then you'll know what it's like to be me inside as well as out.'

Chinese Graveyard

Joel A. Sutherland

Better to light a candle than to curse the darkness
Chinese Proverb

The bar's shade-soaked back corner, ripe with the
odours of poorly circulated and musty air, was the
perfect location for a conversation about death.

Sandra sat in a wicker chair before a table crowded
with empty beer bottles. Across from her sat Bert and
Hannah, a couple older than kerosene, both in their
mid-nineties.

'I'm sure you've heard this one before:
Here lies Lester Moore
Took four slugs from a .44
No less, no more.'

Sandra was absolutely giddy and her excitement was
palpable. She loved nothing more than finding people
who would listen with wide-open ears to her knowledge
of epitaphs. The ironic fact that Bert and Hannah would
probably be lying beneath their own epitaphs within the
year – if not sooner – had not quietened her. All the
same, they did seem interested; their hometown, out in
the sticks north of San Antonio, Texas, was a quiet part
of the country, with few goings-on. A New York writer

blowing into town buying beers and talking of tombstones was a week-making event.

'Yep,' said Bert. He was a short man and he smelled of old potatoes. 'That's one I know. But you're telling me it's real, and not just a joke?'

'Yes, it's real,' said Sandra, ripping the soles of her runners from some mystery goo that had taken up residence on the floor that had clearly never been mopped. 'That one can be found in the Boot Hill Cemetery in Tombstone, Arizona. There are lots of epitaphs that poke fun at people's names, many of them found right here in the southern states.' She raised her forefinger to keep count. 'One: Here Lies Johnny Yeast. Pardon me for not rising.' She raised her middle finger. 'Two: On the 22nd of June Jonathan Fiddle went out of tune.' She raised her ring finger, as excited as a summer picnic. 'And three, my personal favourite, Beza Wood's epitaph:

Here lies one wood
Enclosed in wood.
One wood
Within another.
The outer wood
Is very good.
We cannot praise
The other.'

Bert laughed boyishly, and even Hannah had a hard time maintaining her rigorous façade of imperialness. Sandra took a sip of her Bud Light and smiled. This was the good life. She adored getting away from the manic cavalcade of her daily life in New York. Small town people were good people, and if she left with the knowledge of a few more bizarre tombs, her book of epitaphs would be complete. She eyed Bert and Hannah impishly and tried to sound unassuming. 'So, you two lovebirds have lived here a long time, right? I'll bet you know of some interesting graveyards nearby, something you wouldn't find in a Fodor's travel guide.'

Bert lit up like a Christmas tree, inspiration having struck him. He opened his mouth to proudly answer Sandra's question, but fell grimly silent when he saw his wife glaring at him out of the corner of his eye. His head drooped and he began to peel the label from his beer bottle. Although she was an old pro at it, Hannah never enjoyed cutting her husband's legs out from under him. Her expression softened and she turned to face Sandra. 'Do you know of any epitaphs that would be fitting for this old fart?' she asked, pointing at Bert.

A few came to her mind, but Sandra bit her tongue. Her sense of humour often veered more wildly into the dark than others', and she didn't wish to offend this nice couple who had shared a table with her for the past hour. But she got the feeling that Bert knew of some hidden place that would give her book the sprinkle of sugar that it was sorely lacking. And if Sandra wasn't mistaken she believed that Hannah would let Bert tell her about it if she took a small dig at him. *It's worth a shot*, she thought. 'This epitaph adorns a tombstone in Nova Scotia: Here lies Ezekiel Aikle, age 102. The good die young.'

In a sudden burst of unexpected mirth Hannah laughed for the first time all evening. Bert on the other hand looked sullen for a moment, but quickly warmed to his wife's merriment and was soon laughing alongside her. Hannah looked at Bert through teary eyes and nodded for him to proceed as he wished.

Sandra privately thanked her lucky stars that she had not blown her opportunity with that dig at Bert's age, but she had taken a gamble and it had paid off. Bert set aside his beer and ominously leaned forward, the bones in his back cracking and popping under the strain.

Suddenly, the bar became very quiet. For some unknown reason, Sandra's stomach dipped and she felt a pinch of queasiness strike at her charged nerves.

'There's a place near here, a small private cemetery, that's called the Chinese Graveyard.' Bert glanced at his digital watch face. It read 11:10. 'You go there now, deep into the night, there won't be a soul to bother you. Not a *living* soul, that is.'

Sandra suddenly felt nervous. It was a feeling she was unaccustomed to, even while walking down dark New York streets in the middle of the night. Surprising herself she blurted out, 'Come with me,' and instantly blushed.

'Lady, there ain't enough tea in China to get me anywhere near the Chinese Graveyard after sundown.' Bert paused and chuckled at his unintentional pun.

Sandra, however, didn't laugh. Her skin had begun to prickle and her palms were clammy. *Every time you get goose flesh someone has walked over your future grave,* Sandra reminded herself. She took a timorous sip of her beer and swallowed stiffly.

The thick forest surrounding the road leading to the Chinese Graveyard was menacingly peaceful. The only sound to be heard other than the crunch of dirt and gravel beneath Sandra's tyres was the whispering of the trees in the soft wind.

Drive along until you come to a bend in the road. The graveyard lies just beyond.

Bert's voice lingered in Sandra's mind like an infestation of rats in an attic.

Slow down. Look to your left.

Her brakes squealed as she brought her Porsche to a stop. Sandra did not turn off the ignition. Her headlights illuminated a bright white cross, perhaps seven feet tall, just inside what was unmistakably the lurid locale the old man had sent her to. The cross could be seen through a black wrought iron fence and surrounded by rusty barbed wire. The Texas star sat stoically atop the spikes of the foreboding fence. Was there a name on the cross? It was hard to tell in the pitch-black cover of the night, but there was definitely writing. Sandra squinted and could just barely make out the writing in thick black letters: ST DOMINIQUE.

Kill your ignition. Roll down all four windows. Flash your lights five times. Not four, not six, five. What will happen next will turn your hair grey.

No chance, Sandra thought. *I'm not doing that.* She was spooked enough. And she didn't want to wake anything in the graveyard out of its deep slumber. Not before she got what she came for.

There was a gate in the fence, and it swung open in a burst of choked wind. Sandra bit down on her tongue and cursed as she tasted the warm iron flavour of her own blood.

She wanted to turn around and speed the hell out of there, all the way back to New York, but she felt as if something was prodding her on, encouraging her to walk among the dead. *There's something in there, something for my book, or maybe something else I'm supposed to find for God knows what reason, but there's something in there,* she thought to herself. She didn't want to get back home and regret coming so close only to turn tail and run. That wasn't Sandra Bergdis' style. She turned off the car, flooding her surroundings in shadow, flicked on her flashlight and stepped outside, closing the door as quietly as possible. She held on to the handle a second longer than necessary, then finally walked towards the graveyard.

She paused at the gate. The bright beam of her light sliced through the darkness. She could see makeshift tombstones lining each side of the long run of the cemetery. Thick trees closed in on the grounds, their branches intertwined like writhing tentacles. Down the middle of the cemetery ran a lonely gravel path that came to a dead halt no more than fifty paces beyond the fence. Second thoughts came over Sandra again but she forced her shaking legs to move, and she passed through the gate in trepidation.

Pinned to a high tree on her right was a white sign with

red lettering. Sandra shone the light on it and read the words, immediately wishing she hadn't noticed it. NO WITCHCRAFT – NO SE PERMITE ASER BRUJERIAS AQUI – KEEP OUT – FOR INFO CALL. But there wasn't a number to call for info. She didn't speak Spanish. And witchcraft? What exactly had happened here to necessitate that warning? *Keep walking,* Sandra thought. *Keep moving your feet, right, left, right, left. Find what you came for and burn rubber.*

She finally arrived at the first burial. There was a small archway sheltering a chipped and fading statue of Mother Mary, but in front of that there was very little to signify a body buried below. The grass had long since withered and died, and plastic flowers adorned the ramshackle monument. There were also dolls, garden gnomes and a small clay pig placed around the grave. The pig smiled up at Sandra, its toothy grin welcoming her to its home. Sandra shivered. She scanned the archway for an epitaph but found no markings.

She hesitantly moved on to the next grave, reluctant to fall further into the cemetery. *Further from my car.*

Here she found a rectangular cement frame, roughly five and a half feet long and three feet wide. Leaning against a small wooden cross was a picture, presumably of the dearly departed. But there were three people in the picture, smiling at the camera without any knowledge of the pain and suffering that was barrelling towards their family as unstoppably as a locomotive. A man, a woman, and a teenage boy. Next to the picture was a small bear holding a heart, embroidered with I LOVE YOU MOM. But there were no inscriptions on the cross, and no other notes. Nothing for her book.

It was the third stop that held promise, but it was also the most haunting grave yet. Another wooden cross, two sticks bound with a length of cord, marked the resting place of Guliana Velasquez. Her name was carved into the top of the cross. The dirt in front seemed fresh, as if Guliana had only recently been buried. *Or as if she had to be reburied, ha ha,* Sandra thought to herself, trying to make light of the situation. She immediately regretted it. A light wisp of air slithered underneath her skirt and brushed along her skin from her thighs to her neck, like ethereal fingers tracing her body and searching her soul. There were jagged sticks thrust into the ground along the length of the grave, sticking out at odd angles. To what purpose they served, Sandra could only guess. *To keep people off? Or to keep someone from getting out?* Sandra shook her head and commanded her thoughts to stop turning to ghouls and ghosts. In all her years visiting cemeteries, she had never witnessed anything to make her believe in poltergeists of any kind. And zombies? Forget it. Ridiculous.

The flashlight turned off on its own accord and Sandra swore. She hit it repeatedly with the palm of her hand and it flickered a few times, then finally the batteries caught and the light stayed on.

She saw something move out of the corner of her eye. Sandra spun and flashed the light across the plot. 'Who's there?' she asked the darkness. Silence answered. She glanced back at Guliana Velasquez's grave just as one of the sticks fell from its stance, sending up a tiny cloud of dust.

The ground beneath her very feet groaned as if in great pain and then suddenly the grave before her collapsed, sticks and all, into the earth, creating a deep black chasm. Sandra gasped in a lungful of breathless air and tried to scream but couldn't, her mouth agape and her heart aching, her heart wanting to burst, her heart struggling to squeeze itself into oblivion. A low hum spewed forth from the black hole, the sound infiltrating her head, sharp and merciless, and Sandra felt her sanity slipping away as if it were steam from a kettle. Her fleeing sanity was taking her consciousness with it, the fathomless dark of a coma-like stupor creeping up on her, threatening to make her faint. *Don't pass out,* she urged her body, her soul. *Get out of here!* Her body was numb but finally her feet started to move. She stumbled backwards, never taking her sight off the grave hole, waiting for whatever was within, making that godforsaken hum, to crawl over the lip. And then the world flipped on her as she plummeted backwards, the sky was no longer above her head but below her feet and the ground came rushing up to smack her in the back of the skull. The air was knocked from her lungs and she coughed in pain, trying to figure out what had happened. Above she could see the stars alight in the night, but they were grouped into a rectangular shape. Sandra realised that to her right and her left, her front and her back, were four solid dirt walls, encrusted with a maze of thick roots like varicose veins, scabrous rocks and all sorts of dead things, skin and bones and flesh. She realised with a sickening lurch that she had fallen backwards into an open grave. The demonic humming was louder down in the bowels of the graveyard. The life came back to her voice and she screamed, an ear-piercing scream that filled the grave and the cemetery and the world around her. She forced herself up, tears streaming down her face and leaving black trails of mascara. Scrabbling at the sides of her tomb to pull herself out, Sandra found she was too short; she couldn't reach the top. 'No, no, no,' she repeated over and over as thick wet dirt filled the gaps below her fingernails and stained her clothes. Something grabbed her shoulder from behind and Sandra screamed again, a scream louder than the first, and she dropped to the ground into a fetal position, sheltering her head with her numb pink arms, waiting for the end. But nothing happened. Snivelling, she peered above her trembling flesh and realised that she was still alone in the hole. A tangled root that had brushed her shoulder hung clumsily from the ground near the top of the grave, having come loose in Sandra's panicked scrambling. She stood again and grabbed hold of the root, dug her feet into the dirt as high as she could reach them, and pulled her body up with all of the remnants of her battered strength. She slipped twice and had to regain her purchase, but finally she was able to throw a leg up and over the lip and rolled herself out of the hole. She wasted no time in fleeing from the graveyard, not affording herself a single glance back over her shoulder. She ran as fast as she could back to her car, fumbled for her keys and threw her flashlight on the floor in front of the passenger seat. It blinked on and off once. Sandra sped away in a haze of tyre smoke and skittered gravel.

It only took a few moments for Sandra to control her sobbing, but she knew that it would take a lifetime to control her fear. The surrounding darkness disappeared behind her as she drove northeast, breaking every speeding limit she crossed. The flashlight, rolling back and forth with the bends in the road, flickered twice more.

She remembered her conversation with Hannah and Bert earlier in the evening – *damn you Bert, damn you for sending me to that unholy place* – and felt like it had taken place weeks ago.

Why is it called the Chinese Graveyard? she had asked.

No one knows, at least, no one still living. You'll have to ask that question of the dead.

Sandra shook her head and swallowed dryly. *No thank you.* She hated unsolved mysteries, but she could live quite happily not knowing where the cemetery got its name.

Kill your ignition. Roll down all four windows. Flash your lights five times. Not four, not six, five. What will happen next will turn your hair grey.

What? What will happen?

I've tried to muster the courage to flash my lights in the dark five times. Never could go through with it. The Chinese Graveyard's macabre enough as it is. But it's said that you'll see phantom lights dance from grave to grave, and the air will come alive with the wails of dead souls. You find the cajones to do it, you come back and tell me if it's true.

Sandra's face twisted into a knot and she cursed Bert again. *I didn't need to flash my headlights to raise the dead...*

Sandra swerved to the right around a country corner. The flashlight flared on and off.

A dreadful realisation overcame her and the blood drained from her face. *No, I didn't flash my headlights, but my flashlight flickered just before...just before...*

She didn't want to think of what had happened. *If I ignore it, it doesn't exist.* But the dirt in her fingernails existed, and she could still hear the humming in her ears.

It existed.

Sandra grit her teeth, pushed down on the accelerator, and prayed that whatever it was, whatever it was that existed, whatever it was that had followed her out of the Chinese Graveyard, couldn't keep up with her Porsche.

But she knew no car could outrun a spirit woken from the grave.

The flashlight rolled, bumped and flickered a fifth and final time.

Them Potions I Drank

Brian Rosenberger

Seven days without blinking
Thinking that's not the worst of it
Hair of the werewolf that bit me
Full moon at high noon
A total eclipse of sanity
Mutating and morphing
Something to howl about
Could it be them potions I drank

The glasses never empty
The patrons never leave
Mademoiselle Circe,
the *Mad Lab* mixologist,
Conjures sacrosanct concoctions
She pours 'em red , blue, and chartreuse
Liquids fizz, foam, and sometimes flame
The bubbles tickle my nose
Alchemy and alcohol
A double, I'm in trouble
A signal for last call so

Call security, the military, maybe a priest
Make it the morgue the merrier
Somebody better call the wife
'Cause I won't be crawling home tonight
Head playing hopscotch

What have I become
Every night the same routine
Monster stagger
Unholy swagger
Another massacre in *Margaritaville*
Chemistry can be dangerous
And delicious
So smooth going down
Who's been sleeping in my flesh
This Jekyll can't Hyde
Second skin shed but
Still a bit long in the tooth
Hangover haunting me
Blame it on them potions I drank

In the Cinema Tree
with Orbiting Heads

Kek-W

For a while I lived in the bole of a tree in Swallow Arms Park.

Why did I do it? I've no idea, really. Suffice to say that it suited me at the time. I crawled inside, one afternoon in the autumn, and decided to stay. Looking back now, I wonder if I had been searching for somewhere dark and quiet to die. The idea of my hidden corpse being discovered several months later, mummified and bejewelled with frozen dew, still fills me with a certain grim satisfaction.

The entrance was a narrow, rabbit-sized arch half hidden in a warped tangle of roots where the base of the tree had rotted away. To enter, I had to jack-knife my body at an awkward angle up inside the trunk. The rough grain of the wood grazed my knuckles, and splinters ripped my cheeks as I pulled myself backwards and up into the tree's musty interior. The exertion and this sudden, unexpected invasion of sensation into my own muted inner-life seemed to reinvigorate me.

The tree was a very snug fit, so I was forced to stand

upright. I could crouch a little with difficulty, but sitting was impossible. I found that if I stood with my feet about two foot apart then they were completely invisible to the outside world.

If my subconscious had been seeking death, then my new surroundings quickly acted as an antidote. It was pleasantly warm within the tree and the wood gave off a calming aroma that was exotic yet comfortingly familiar. Although the hollow was narrow and restrictive, there was also something womb-like and sensual about being confined within the tree, as if I was wearing the skin of some vast, alien creature.

When I had entered, the late afternoon light had been grainy and dull, almost monochrome. Inside it was now completely dark, so my initial explorations were sightless. I slowly rubbed my fingers up and down the tree's inner skin as if it were a Braille map of the moon. I followed its curves and wrinkled contours, across lignified craters and ridges, discovering patches that were curiously smooth and bereft of texture. Elsewhere, I found a soft tuft of moss or brittle scabs of lichen that powdered at my touch. Polypore fungi hung from the wall, as wrinkled and leathery as an old woman's breasts.

There were knobs and buds of twisted wood that felt like the fossilised remains of organic machinery; recesses and crevasses of varying sizes that could accommodate a finger or a fist. In one, I found an ancient clump of cobweb; in another, a small nest of ants. Each was quickly memorised by my sensation-famished body.

Beneath my feet was a fibrous mulch of soil and decaying vegetable matter. Above was a ceiling of sorts, honeycombed by decades of decay. Here, the wood had softened into stalactites that crumbled like ancient books, showering me with insects and damp sawdust. The air was ripe with the odour of rot, like the atmosphere of some exotic lost world. I felt an inexplicable sense of elation. Paradoxically, the physical restrictions imposed by the tree seemed to open up an endless vista of possibilities.

At first, my legs spasmed with cramp. Later, I found I could turn a full circle if I was careful. I soon learned, after a couple hundred turns, how to subtly dip and twist without scraping my head or an elbow. The desire to writhe within the tree was oddly addictive. The place seemed to induce me to move in a certain manner as if my sinews were mimicking the whorls in the woodgrain or the movement of the branches outside.

The wood creaked and groaned as the biomass above me swayed in the wind, tugging at the trunk below. I heard muffled bird-noise as crows and wood-pigeons dreamed of blood-bloated worms and cackled in their sleep. Wood-boring beetles ticked deep within ancient layers of xylem.

But when the moon rose, something miraculous happened. A pale, ghostly image of the outside world appeared on the wood just above my head. A painting made from light that flickered uncertainly, like an old kino. It was upside-down, but I could clearly make out the screen of trees which hid the nearby recycling plant.

I soon discovered that the image was being captured through a minute hole in the tree-trunk. Whether this was artificial or not, I could not say, but the interior of the tree acted like a camera obscura, a pinhole camera through which Swallow Arms Park could be surreptitiously observed.

As the moon crept across the sky, this phantom projection slid over the wood-grain, changing its perspective like an impossibly slow tracking shot. And whenever the moon was obscured by clouds the scene would suddenly fade out, mimicking a cinematic dissolve.

I watched as a dark, hulking form, possibly a badger, emerged from beneath a tree. It scuttled off on all-fours across a flower bed, disappearing into the pool of shadows behind the play area. An eerie, strangulated cry echoed across the park.

The scene shifted in and out of focus as if I was watching an experimental film shot by some forgotten Czechoslovakian director. Edited by random cloud cover, it cut between spectral, muted greys and crystal-sharp neorealist noir.

I watched as a woman approached the tree, her face gaunt and chalk-white, as if she had somehow escaped from a silent 1920s melodrama. I tried to twist my neck to get a better view of her pale, inverted head, but a sudden, uncontrollable tremor of lust swept upwards from my lower bowel and I found myself wriggling back out through the narrow hole and into the chill night air.

I stumbled to my feet and she smiled at me, horribly, with her thin, bloodless lips. Black hair hung limply from her scalp. She walked backwards, slowly and self-consciously, as though she was reversing through a minefield. She beckoned me to follow her, making arcane gestures with some nonsensical contraption built from Sprite cans and twisted car-radio aerials.

Her limbs were meatless and bony, but a fierce hunger burned deep within her eyes. She was draped in the torn, grease-smeared uniform of a local supermarket chain. On her breast was a badge that read: 'Sarah Holt. Customer Services.' Her arms and the hollows of her mouth and eyes were stained with blackberry juice. From her dishevelled appearance I gauged that she had been living wild in the park for some months.

She led me back to her tree, rattling her ridiculous wire-frame fetish and making wet, clicking noises with her tongue. Most of her teeth were gone and she smelled like an old fox, but the sight of her emaciated body aroused me on some vague, abstract level. Thin and pallid, her grey, twig-like limbs reminded me of a miniature tree stripped of its leaves by the elements.

She said something in a language that might have once been English. Her voice was rough as old stone, but seemed to form a question. She crouched down to show me the moss-furred entrance to her own secret den and then exposed herself.

Her husband ran at me from the bushes, shrieking like a neutered gelding. He swung at me with a wooden fence post, but missed my head, catching me instead on the shoulder.

His hair was long, filthy and matted, as was his beard.

He had plaited them with sweet wrappers and bits of coloured string. Around his neck he wore a necklace of pigeon feathers, acorns and cats' bones. He snarled and spat at me like a dog with distemper, recklessly swinging his makeshift club. I should have been terrified, but I wasn't. Instead, I felt strangely *inconvenienced*. I realised now that I had been deliberately lured here and ambushed, but their motives, if they even had any, were of little interest to me. Now that the promise of a sexual liaison had been withdrawn, I merely wished to return to the pin-hole camera tree.

I jumped back as he swung at me again. My shoulder throbbed from where he'd struck me. His wife giggled and squealed her encouragement. Irritated, I kicked out at him and caught him in the shins. He seemed confused by my counter-attack, as if this was an option he had never considered. Our encounter had invigorated me, whereas he seemed a little sluggish. I was not physically strong, but I was determined to resist him as best as I could.

I rammed into him with my shoulder, knocking him off balance. I punched him, somewhat limply I thought, with my left fist and he grunted like a pig. Two men fighting while a woman looked on: it seemed so ludicrously clichéd, so pathetically mock-heroic that I wanted to laugh, yet the moment was somehow also entrenched in the eternal.

A soft-drink can clattered as he stumbled over the arcane tin-and-wire device that his wife had fashioned. He recoiled, as if in horror, so I snatched it up and shook it at him, half intending to use it as a weapon.

He backed away and I realised that the object held some terrifying significance for him. I rattled it, taunting him with it. There was a genuine look of fear on his grime-encrusted face as he retreated to a safe distance. I spat at the ground, contemptuously, then turned and walked away.

He unexpectedly launched himself at me from behind and we both crashed through a flimsy fence into the play area. I rolled off to one side and he thankfully parted company with my back. The metal contraption was lost somewhere in the shadows.

He let out an awful, animal-like howl and chased me under a climbing frame and back around the roundabout. Desperate to find a weapon, I grabbed the wooden seat of a swing with both hands and hit him in the side of the head as hard as I could. There was a terrible crack and he fell sideways against the swing's rust-mottled frame, then slid limply to the ground.

I kicked him in the head a few times, but failed to elicit a response. So I jumped on his back and the air left his lungs with a grotesque sigh.

His wife had retreated back into her tree, where she made muffled high-pitched noises that sounded like a frightened cat. I reached in and grabbed at her ankles to forcibly pull her out, but she had disappeared up inside the trunk beyond my reach.

Her husband's possessions, I decided, were now mine by right. I recalled how I had earlier mistaken him for an animal emerging from his den and realised that he too must have inhabited a tree.

I rooted through the wet grass, pulling back dock-leaves until I exposed the hidden entrance to his hidey-hole. A dull red light leaked out from within. As I pushed my head through into the tree, I found the hollow was lit by an old bicycle-lamp. Decorated by a glittering mosaic of broken glass and damp collages torn from old girly-mags, his sanctum resembled a fantastic crimson-tinted grotto. But I only caught the most fleeting of glimpses.

My head caught on something – a fishing line, I think – and a booby trap was triggered. He had weighted down the sharpened head of a garden spade with a breeze block, and this fell on my throat, partially severing my head.

My line of vision flipped backwards into an impossible new position. I would have cried out, but I no longer had a voice. Or even the need for one.

Blood sprayed across my face, horizontally, a flat sheet of liquid that darkened my world with its touch and dragged me down into a narrow corridor wallpapered by memories. I hurtled through my past at impossible velocities and, when there was no more oxygen left to fuel my neurons, I exited myself through the crown chakra.

The woman made a soft mewling sound as she pulled at my feet, but my spine was still lodged under the spade. Later, she stripped my corpse and stuffed me, pale and bloody, into yet another tree. Here, I was slowly smoked over a tiny fire of hazel and chestnut twigs, and left to hang while she butchered and ate me at her own lei-sure.

The body of her dead husband she returned to his tree untouched, slowing turning it into a surreptitious shrine over the following months. My own disembodied head now orbits the Cinema Tree, so that I am forced to watch her ridiculous nocturnal rituals as I bob up and down on the autumn wind like a child's balloon. I am an earthbound spirit now; a hapless phantom head trapped by the tree's supernatural gravity and unable to reach my necessary escape velocity. It binds me here like glue, its branches twisted into some implausible three-dimensional sigil that attracts me like a spiritual magnet.

There are at least three dozen of us, bodiless spirit-heads whose orbits weave in and out of each other's flight paths like the moons of Jupiter. Her husband's head follows me constantly, tracking my trajectory, snarling and hissing ecto-spectral spittle like a rabid rottweiler, his phantom breath forever hot on my neck.

The others here howl and leer and weep, their faces like blotchy old cauliflowers as they drift past me, lit by the endless glare of infrared night. Every tree in the park has grown into its own awful configuration, each with a particular aspect or darkly ascendant trait: the one housing my own mortal remains is called The Carvery and glows at night with a halo of blue arterial light that resembles deoxygenated blood.

With my new eyes I can now see how each tree's unique branch structure has subtly warped the physical space around it, casting an addictively malign influence over the world of the living. Any day now, I'm sure, the Cinema Tree will attract a new unwitting inhabitant and the show will begin once more.

Wendy

Ryan Cooper

Roger started stirring, then let out a moan and coughed what I think was a tooth on to the floor, where it drifted in the puddle of blood pooling from his smashed lips. He started toward consciousness, but I still had a lot of places to look and the sounds burbling from his mouth made it so I couldn't think, so I kicked him again, this time across the bridge of his nose.

I saw Wendy again. She was a girl about 12 years old, I think, at the Laundromat, helping her mother fold towels and put them in a basket. I didn't even know it was Wendy at first; I didn't know what to look for. I was reading a newspaper story about a new vegetarian restaurant on 5th and I happened to glance up and catch her eye. When I realised it was Wendy, the ringing in my ears got so loud I couldn't concentrate. I closed my eyes tight for a while, until it got quiet. When I could focus again, she was gone.

'Make your birthday wish into this box.' Wendy was pulling out a big pink hatbox.

'Does that make it come true?' I asked. On your 9th birthday wishes are still pretty big. I was debating on using it for either a bike or a rocket ship, knowing one was more realistic than the other, but not wanting to risk wasting the power of the wish on the mundane.

'I don't know if it helps it come true,' she said, 'but it makes some of the magic stay in the box, and makes this a magic box. I've been storing wishes and magic stuff in here for a long time.'

I think the next time I found Wendy after she left me was at the grocery store, loading apples into a cart. After the Laundromat, I had been watching for her, but I was still unprepared for the clamour in my head when I saw her. She was maybe 30 years old now, and a blonde. It was a new look for her, but it really suited her face right now. This time, I only got one good look at her before I had to press my palms against my eyes until the noise and pressure subsided.

In the guest room I find a dresser that might be the one, so I open each drawer and pour the contents out.

Sweaters, sweaters, sweaters, man, Wendy and Roger have a lot of sweaters...but it's not there either. I'm beginning to get mad and I think I will kick Roger in the stomach as I pass through the kitchen again – just for the hell of it.

Worlds move quickly when you're a kid. Before I knew it I was 10 and my parents moved to Tennessee. Moving away from Wendy was hard. She was my neighbour and my best friend. I didn't like girls, but Wendy didn't count. We wrote letters; short scrabbling sloppy transcripts that broke down the daily events of a 10-year-old kid:

Dear Wendy,

How are you? I am fine. Today I saw a snake under the porch. My mom says maybe we can come back to Michigan in June for my birthday. I hope so. How is school? My teacher is nice.

Your friend,

Jeffrey

Wendy's responses were similarly exciting. I ran home from school every day hoping a letter would be there.

I am getting really frustrated now. Wendy is duct-taped to a chair in the bedroom, and I just want to sit and talk to her, find out how all this happened, and why she left, but every time I go in there, she is either glaring at me from behind the tape on her mouth, or sobbing, her shoulders heaving. I try to tell it will be OK, we just need to talk, sort things out, but the way her eyes panic when I try to talk to her makes the whining sound in my ears get so loud that I want to throw up, and I have to leave the room again, and keep looking, always looking; I've been here over an hour, and I'm still fucking looking.

The worst day was the day I saw Wendy twice. I was walking out of the post office when I saw her pulling out of the parking lot. The years had not been kind. She had a creased face that looked 50 but may not have even been 35. My head started throbbing and I sat down on the kerb. After the pain calmed enough for me to stand again, I started walking in the direction her car had gone and I saw her again, 18 or so and blonde once more, walking a big yellow dog down the pavement. Seeing her twice so close together made my head hurt so much worse this time. I stumbled slightly, actually tripping off the kerb before catching myself. I put my hands on my thighs, hunched over, taking deep breaths and collecting myself. After I calmed down a bit, she was gone again.

I did get to spend my 11th birthday with Wendy, and my 12th. She showed me that she saved every letter I'd written her; they were in the hatbox with the birthday wishes.

And, on both those birthdays, I made my wish into that box again. The box had to be getting more magical, because I wished as hard as I ever had on those birthdays. And while I don't know if the box helped my wishes come true, they didn't hurt; in April of the next year, my Dad's company sent him back to Michigan, and Wendy and I lived within a few blocks of one another again.

The tiny apartment is in a shambles now. I have torn apart every cabinet, emptied every drawer, overturned the furniture, even. A large lamp is shattered down the whole length of the hall, and the shards are crunching like hard candy under my shoes as I pace back and forth from room to room. Roger has stirred and been beaten down several times; I really feel bad for the guy, he didn't ask for this. If he'd just stay out and let me take care of what doesn't concern him, all of us could get on with our lives. He just doesn't get it, and Wendy is being selfish.

Another cruel day was the day that Wendy talked to me. I was sitting on a bench in the mall enjoying a cup of coffee, and she was walking by, doing one of those mall power-walking things. She looked like a suburban soccer mom, hair pulled back in a ponytail, sexy in an odd domestic sort of way; again, not the way I pictured Wendy wanting to be, but I was apparently bad at this game. I was watching her quietly pass, the pain was a dull throb – I was learning how to choke it back by then; I was actually getting better at it. Then she smiled, winked and said a cheery 'H'lo!' and the flashing started behind my eyes again. I sat stock still for minutes, calming myself, willing my vision back. After I had calmed, I could still see her walking way down the mall, and I got up and left before she made her return trip.

We were about to graduate high school when Wendy got sick the first time. I was 17. She had just turned 18. By that time we had kissed, gone to prom together, and clumsily lost our virginity to one another on a couch in her parent's garage. It felt weird, but right. We decided that maybe we were better off as friends, but somehow we managed to have sex a lot more times after that. So then we decided we'd be friends who had sex, and then we just gave up on that idea and she let me call her 'baby' and 'my girlfriend'.

I am trying to calm Wendy down now so I can take the tape off her mouth and we can talk. She is glaring, angry and frightened at the same time, and she is trying to pull away when I try to brush her hair out of her eyes. I want to grab her and pull her close and kiss her forehead and stroke her hair and tell her shhhh baby, it's OK, I don't know why you left and I don't care but it's OK and we're together now and I understand that you've moved on; that's OK but can't we talk for a while, and she won't even let me brush her hair out of her eyes! This isn't right, and it isn't fair, but I really just need to calm the fuck down before I walk in to the kitchen and just beat Roger to death for taking her, which isn't his fault, so I'm just going to stand here and breathe for a minute.

After another week or two, I learned to keep it in check, and started realising Wendy was around much more than I thought at first. I could sense her without seeing her; I knew to look where she'd be, and to ready myself for the assault on my senses that occurred when we connected, when we locked eyes. I could return her glance, and even though I wasn't ready to talk to her – it hurt too much – I realised that she must still care. She could be anywhere right now, and more often than not she would be near me. At one minute she might be the infant in the shopping cart to my right, and a few minutes later she was a teenage girl stocking the pineapples in the produce section. She was close to me all the time, glancing at me from behind these faces, letting me see her, letting me know she's there.

I was 22 when Wendy left me. It wasn't sudden; she'd been slowly getting sicker for almost five years by then. It was still earth shattering, like waking up one day to find the walls of your room gone. I couldn't believe that this girl who had been part of my life this whole time could simply not be anymore. I sat with her in the hospital as her kidneys gave up, hugged her mom and cried, went to the funeral and tried to figure out what came next. It was hard to figure out; not having Wendy felt like some-body had reached into my guts and took out a hunk, leaving just empty space that needed to be filled.

It's simply not here. I have torn this apartment apart, and it's not here. I do realise what I need to do. As hard as it is on me, it really is time to go to the source. I need to talk to Wendy.

After I realised that Wendy was always close, Wendy stayed in one spot. Wendy was the girl who worked at the drug-store where I filled my prescriptions, bought cigarettes and even got my groceries when I didn't feel like taking the bus downtown. She had been there for a few years, I remembered her, but she had only been Wendy for a few days. And she talked to me! This was new; I was talking to Wendy again without my stomach churning. And it was nice.

'Hey Hon,' and 'come back soon,' and 'do you want your receipt with you or in the bag?' Trivialities, nothings coming from red lips and chubby cheeks but I could see Wendy behind those eyes, and I was happy, but I missed her and needed to know why she left.

Wendy's parents could remember the pink hatbox but they didn't know where it was. Her dad said he hadn't seen it in years. I know this wasn't true, this was too important. I wasn't superstitious but if anything was magical, it was this box filled with birthday wishes and love letters, and even after my doctor told me to stop 'fixating on this object' and to 'move forward with life', I never forgot about it.

'Wendy? I'm going to take the tape off your mouth, and you won't scream. We'll just talk, OK?' There is a high whining buzz in my ears, but it's soft enough now that I am able to sit calmly next to Wendy on the bed.

She nods. Snot is running from her nose across the surface of the tape. I grab the edge of the tape, tell her I'm sorry, and yank the tape off swiftly to shorten the discomfort.

'Why are you... Roger... What are you...?' She starts to cry.

'Shhhhhh, baby girl, shhhhh, Wendy, I just need to

know why? Why'd you go? Just tell me why and we can start over. You're back and that's what's important...'

'I'm not... I don't know what... What happened to Roger?'

'Wendy, calm down, we're sorting this out. Roger will be OK. I'm going to take you home.'

'Please, I don't know why you're doing this, I'm not Wendy. I don't know Wendy. My name is Janice. Please...'

'STOP IT!' And I did it. I slapped her. I struck Wendy in anger and the impact of that slap echoed through my arm and into my head where it thrummed, deep and loud, like an old lawnmower, loud, sputtering, painful. 'Wendy, stop it. This is too important.'

'I'm not Wendy.' She sounds so sad that I want to believe her. For a minute I do. Then she looks up at me, and I see Wendy in her eyes. And I feel awful. This girl isn't Wendy. Wendy is inside this girl, trying to get back to me. There's no magic in a box of letters, the magic is how much Wendy loved me, loves me, how hard she's trying to get back to me, and I've been too fucking selfish to help her get back. My head doesn't hurt so much now.

'Roger, wake up!'

He moans as I slightly slap his face. I think I can feel his jaw is broken from where I hit him. I kind of feel bad about that. His eyes are glazed, but he's aware.

'Can you hear me?'

He nods pitifully.

'Good. I'm really sorry about this Rog, but I needed you to see this. You need to know. I'm not here to hurt you guys, and if you don't see this you won't understand.'

I've dragged him in to the bedroom. I tried to drag Wendy out to him at first, but the chair she was bound to was too heavy; her hair came out in a fistful when I tried to pull her down the hall. So I brought Roger back here.

'Listen guys, I'm really sorry for doing this to you. None of this your fault. You two don't deserve this. But neither did I, and I have a chance to get her back, and be happy again. It's not fair. None of this is. But I have to help Wendy get back. Watch. Just watch for a minute. You'll understand when you see.'

I showed him what was in my hand – a piece of the broken lamp a little longer than my fist. Then I grabbed Wendy's cheek with my other hand, and pushed the piece of glass under the skin along her jaw. Moving my hand up and down, I began to slice away all of the parts that weren't Wendy. We all screamed.

Extensions

Andrew Tisbert

Vivian broke up with Miles right there on his front steps. They had walked out of the dark house together. Sure, they had been fighting, but Miles was still surprised when, instead of allowing him to grasp her pale hand, she rolled her eyes and backed down the supple marble steps that gave slightly beneath their feet. Afterward, he could remember clearly the sound of the jay birds and cardinals chirping Beethoven from within his lush gardens as she spoke, their soft lips smacking.

'We are through,' she said.

He looked up at the dimming sky, all strands of sable, silver and gold. He looked over her shoulder at his driveway that tunnelled away to the street through the waving fingers and vines of his gardens. Yes, he could remember every detail. He finally met the hard, black gaze of those eyes.

'You're going to throw this away? All this time together, wasted...'

'It's only been two months, Miles.'

'But I love you. You are the one.' In retrospect his

words sounded whiny and desperate even to him. Not his shining moment.

Her little hand flew up and flitted in front of her. 'You know what? I don't care. You scare me. Your house scares me. I'm out of here.' And with that she turned and headed down the driveway. Miles dug his toes into the fleshy front landing and watched her little body grow smaller in the distance, the heads of lavender and vermillion tulips turning to follow, smelling her for him as she passed. And she was gone. Every detail. He remembered every detail.

Of course, it helped that the house remembered it for him. Each impression was recorded. The look of her white skin and every freckle. The mild spice of sweat from her groin within the laced summer dress. Her blood pressure, her heart thumping – she really *was* afraid. He went into the review room and watched the whole thing happen again, over and over. He watched it happen from every angle. He smelled every wafting breeze. He felt the flush in his own cheeks, watched it rise on his face. He listened to the stuttering uncertainty of his responses, the high pitch of his voice. It was awful. Why was this happening? Miles was a catch. He was beautiful and rich and sensitive. He was always carefully mindful of others. He spent hours every day analysing his behaviour in the review room, just to improve himself, to be open to self-discovery. It didn't make any sense. He pulled off his shirt and flexed. One of the room's panels immediately reflected the image of his tanned, rippling body. For a while he watched the veins stick out on his biceps and chest and it made him feel a little better. His automatic bed was working – a sheen of health glowed from his flesh; every muscle was raised in perfect proportion. Lately he'd found himself staring down at his immaculate six-pack to get off while he slid himself in and out of Vivian. And in the review room it was his own face he focused on when he watched their lovemaking. There, when he half-closed his eyes. That's when he'd been thinking about the big-breasted brunette at the All Market. And that little twitch, that was a brief moment of guilt overlaying strands of pleasure. It was amazing what your own face could tell you about yourself, and most people never watched it. There was so much uncertainty and confusion in any normal person's head. Just a little reflective scrutiny could teach so much. And then, when you saw how you looked, how you acted, you could grow to understand the array, the tangled mass of misunderstandings that made up each interaction of every day. Ah, *that's* how your face looked when you were thinking about the comment she made about your house. There, that half smile the last time you had sex made her think you liked the way she moved her hips just then – but you really only wanted to reassure her while you thought about something else, because that little motion sort of annoyed you. Interactions were so convoluted. It took daily meditation and scrutiny to better oneself, to understand, to gain the control that could nurture clarity.

'All right. I've had enough for now,' he told the review room. The panels instantly switched to his favorite channel. The screens filled with ad images of perfect men and women, idealized form and motion. Even their sweat was perfect. Miles was making himself into those images, because he had the money to do it. And he made no excuses for it.

He went out the back door to his meat garden, where phallic growths of his own flesh hung from their branches. This was part of his self-improvement as well. He was a vegetarian – he only ate himself. He cut a slab down, peeled off its skin, and brought it to the indoor grill in the kitchen.

Miles owed his fortune to the extinction of the great silver back gorillas and the brief popularity of mobile phones. In the jungles of the Congo, now long gone, rebel forces held their base of operation for many years and controlled mines that produced an ore – he couldn't remember what they called the stuff – that was necessary to manufacture mobile phones. The rebels sold this ore to finance their operations until the world learned they were also slaughtering gorillas for food at a startling pace and every mobile phone manufacturing company vowed not to purchase from them. That's where Miles' great-grandfather, Roddy Usher, came in. He did business with the rebels, so the mobile phone companies could say they held no association with them. Everyone came out on top – made a killing, so to speak. And when Miles turned of legal age he could afford the internal modifications that allowed him to operate this house, this extension of himself. It was pleasingly ironic, when Miles thought about it. Now mobile *phones* were extinct and every zoo in the world had its own pack – is that what they were called? – of cloned gorillas. Things had come around full circle. And Miles had a mansion that was a part of him, a house designed to nurture his own personal growth, to *perfect* him. To be an additional right hand. It was a great gift, and he needed it badly right now.

For the next three days he found himself in the review room almost constantly. He watched himself carefully, through every interaction with Vivian that had ever occurred on the mansion grounds. He tried to see himself as Vivian saw him. He watched every word he had spoken to her. The review room could show him how he felt viscerally at the time, as well as how he sounded and appeared and smelled and felt from the outside. He tried to see what Vivian meant when she said he scared her. He went over every blink, every sniff. There, you said how pretty the flowers were when she touched a petal of one of your indigo roses and it flinched. Was your inflection somehow *off* right there? Did it imply a sarcasm you did not intend? Were you condescending? Wait, no, you remember what you were thinking when your eyelids flickered. You thought she was pleased; you were showing her your sensitive side. And you were so beautiful. Your bed's intermittent ultraviolet lights and sonic fields that stimulated every muscle and controlled the nano-injections and conducted the auto repairs of your bodily systems were working magnificently. You were like the celebrities on vision. Every twitch and turn was idealized. You couldn't help watch yourself in awe the supple way you moved, the subtle turns of expression that emerged on the tan sea of your face. Why couldn't Vivian see *this*? This is what you truly are. Miles decided it was important to present that graceful, perfect self-image. After all, that had to be what Vivian saw in him in the first place. Setting the perfect line of his jaw, he went outside and sat on the front steps. He tapped his ear and called her.

Her black hair was dishevelled and her eyes were bloodshot when she answered.

'Have you been crying?' he asked.

'Why should you care?'

Miles sighed. 'I care more than you know, Viv. You are all I can think about.'

She must have wanted to hear something like that, because her expression shifted involuntarily. 'Really?' she said. And that's when the conversation began in earnest, all defences down. And somehow Miles convinced her to come over one more time and...talk about things. After he tapped his ear again to end the call he sat there thinking.

What had caused her to change her mind? Clearly, he had done something right. He raised an arm and one of the cardinals landed on his wrist. They regarded each other for a series of slow, deep breaths. 'You should watch what you did in the review room before she gets here,' said the bird.

'You're right. Maybe I can figure it out.' And he went inside.

But Miles *couldn't* figure it out. Sure, he recognised he'd told Vivian what she wanted to hear – how he missed her so much, how he thought about her constantly, how he remembered every moment they were together so perfectly, with such clarity. But that wasn't enough by way of explanation. He scrutinised himself for the key, for what caused her to believe him, to trust him one more time. Finally he gave up and paced his house while he waited for her.

Wandering through the great building soothed him. It was like making his way through his own insides. He slid down hallways like his own corpuscles through interconnected veins. He stopped in various rooms – the library upstairs like a great stomach full of knowledge, digesting books for him and accessing the information directly to his brain if he asked for it; the massive dining room arched like an extra mouth. He took the elevator downward into his bowels. He could feel his own life all around him, the thunderous pulse aching in his ears. When Vivian finally stood on the tongue of his front step, he felt her there. She didn't even have to ring the doorbell. The house reflected his excitement and the door opened up for her on its own. Miles hurried back upstairs to greet her. And right away he knew something was wrong. She gave him an odd look even before he hugged her and kissed her ear lobe and begged her forgiveness. He suppressed the anger that look stirred up.

Miles led her into the sitting room. He was aware of the beams along the walls rising up like a set of ribs.

They almost seemed to creak with every breath he took. Actually, it calmed his nerves as he took Vivian's hand and led her to the couch in front of the picture glass window that overlooked the meat garden.

'You see, this is the problem,' said Vivian.

Miles raised a perfect eyebrow.

'I can tell when you've sunk into this place, Miles. Don't you get it?'

'Viv, this house is just a tool, like my hand.' He raised a fist for emphasis.

'No. It's like you are disappearing into your own self. You don't see anything else.'

'I see you.'

She shook her head sadly. 'No you don't. Or maybe you do, but only in relation to how I affect you. Do you even know what my new job is, or my favorite colour?'

Miles looked out the window and tried to access the review room files without being too conspicuous. The sky had grown grey. 'Aqua blue. And you grow eyes for the All Market.'

'The house just told you those things, Miles. Do you think I'm stupid?'

That earlier anger re-asserted itself. Miles felt it shaking through the walls. He turned back to Vivian with a slow, cold grace. 'This house *is* me. It is a part of my body and my mind. It is my tutor and my protector. It is my self-discovery.'

'No, Miles. That's an illusion. You are confused by a conglomeration of bio-cybernetics, nanos and surro-genetics. I think you were a nice guy once, you know that?

But you've been sinking a little deeper every day since I've met you. I can't be around to watch it.'

'This is what I get for having a mind to improve myself? To analyse myself toward deeper self-knowledge? You wouldn't think that would be a crime, now would you?'

'All right. You know what?' She jerked upright from the couch. It began to rain outside; big amber drops streaked the window. 'I knew this was a mistake. I never should have come here again. Goodbye, Miles. And this time I mean it for good.'

Looking back on the whole scene through the review room, Miles could see that he knew he wasn't thinking clearly even as it happened. But that anger had taken hold, and he knew that if she left this time, it really *was* going to be for good.

She cried out when he yanked her arm, but the house was able to silence the screams. He dragged her to the elevator and shoved her in. The house knew what to do. It took her down into the bowels. It sedated her and softened a swath of floor for a mattress and laid her down. And the basement doors locked themselves.

In the meantime, Miles had some studying to do. He sat down in the womb of the review room, and began watching himself with renewed fervour. Clearly, he had missed something. He had misunderstood how she could have misunderstood him. She responded to that misunderstanding, and their relationship spiralled out of control from there. Now he had to figure it out, so he could get her out of the basement and make things right between them.

But after several hours he ground his teeth in frustration. It had stopped raining outside and he left the review room to open a window in the kitchen. The birds were singing Handel's Messiah. It was quite unimpressive in their high-pitched little voices. He was still missing something - the most *important* something. You've watched yourself over and over, and you still miss it. As impossible as that seems, you still miss it. If only you could *see* yourself missing it, then you could...

The anger that had brought him to this point had long ago dissipated. Miles was left with a hollow feeling in his stomach. He was worried about Vivian downstairs, all alone. If she misunderstood him before, what would she be thinking now? He hoped she wasn't frightened. But the only solution now was to find the understanding that had so eluded him. He went back into the review room and watched himself until the images he saw of his face, the motion of his well-muscled arms, turned into a dream.

Miles awoke with the review room still bombarding him with images of himself. Three of his garden birds had flown in through the kitchen window and flitted around his head, two bright red, and a rich clean blue. They perched on him as soon as he raised his arm. They stared at him, miniature images of his face. But it was Vivian's voice he heard when they spoke in unison. She sounded weak, as if the sedatives hadn't quite worn off.

'Miles,' said the birds. 'Miles, where are you?'

'Quiet, now,' he told them. 'It will be all right.'

'Miles, I'm scared. It's dark. Please let me out.'

'Don't worry, Vivian. I just need some time to figure this out. I'll fix things. I promise.'

'What are you going to do to me?'

'I'm going to figure things out, I said.' He shook the birds off his arm in frustration. A heavy sense of embarrassment and regret was settling into the flesh and bone of the house. He felt it everywhere, like an infection. Miles touched his forehead and wondered if he had a fever. Vivian was making him sick. He had to figure things out before his immune system kicked in. You should feed her down there, and then give her another sleeping injection, he thought. And the house did.

Two more days brought him no success. As night settled around the house and he willed on the lights in the review room he remembered listening to the birds sing The Messiah in the kitchen, so he reviewed himself listening. It seemed as if some revelation had begun to transform his face. What had he been thinking? He had been thinking about the fact that he was still missing something. And that it might be helpful...to *watch* himself miss it. Of course. Miles wondered why, in all this time he hadn't thought of it.

A cardinal was flying frantically around the room. 'Help me,' it sang. 'Please help me. Miles. Can you hear me? Miles. I'm sorry. I'll do anything. Just let me out...'

Miles began running reviews again, only this time he watched himself watching reviews. There, you were surprised by that expression on your face when you saw your anger ignite at the sad look she gave you in the doorway. There, an expression of fear came over you when you watched yourself grab Vivian by the arm. Yes. Things would be even clearer now.

'Miles, please forgive me. I'll do anything you want. I'm bleeding. I tried to pry the elevator open and I've cut myself. Please.'

'Go to sleep,' he told the bird. She *was* an infection inside him. Or a tumour. He told the house to begin treating the disease.

In the meantime, he had studying to do. Who knew what revelations were ahead, as he analysed himself analysing himself? It was like peeling an onion. Maybe he would have to watch reviews of what he was doing even now. Like looking into mirrors reflecting mirrors. There were depths within depths here. Now he was getting somewhere.

The birds began The Messiah again.

Murder for Breakfast

Oren Shafir

Ed crashes into his chair – waves of fat jiggling from the jowls of his neck and arms down to his belly, thighs and calves – and demands coffee; Janet thumps a mug of scalding liquid next to his plate.

Ed opens the *Herald* with great fanfare and settles in behind it; Janet takes advantage of his blocked vision to open the cabinet drawer on the wall next to her and pick up the Smith and Wesson inside it.

Ed slurps loudly into his coffee mug as if making rapacious love; Janet moans murmurs of affection to the gun in her hand.

Ed spits out a cacophony of phrases about the Dodgers, peppered by a slew of words with hard consonants; Janet strokes the gun fondly.

Ed pronounces his three-step plan for peace in the Middle East and the eradication of terrorism (if only the idiots would listen); Janet reaches for the cartridge and the silencer in the drawer.

Ed chews his English muffin audibly; Janet quietly loads the gun and attaches the silencer.

As the alarm on Ed's wristwatch starts beeping shrilly, he shouts, '7:30, some of us have to get to work, you know,' and then guffaws at his little joke; Janet aims at where she thinks the middle of Ed's forehead is behind the newspaper, exhales and slowly pulls the trigger.

As Ed grunts and falls backwards, his head bounces off the wall and then falls forward and smacks the table, and his blood oozes from underneath the newspaper toward the table edge, thick and red; Janet smiles.

Ed arises with a flourish, pulling his thin black comb from his back pocket, and combs the remaining strands of his pale blond hair over his pink head; Janet follows him as he walks to the door and presses her thin lips to his flabby cheeks.

Ed guns the Land Rover and takes off to work; Janet walks back to the table and mimes unscrewing the silencer, removing the cartridge and placing the gun carefully in the drawer – ready for tomorrow.

Blind Spot

Jamie Killen

'**B**eing dead doesn't mean being invisible, girl; it means being ignored.'

I remember Leonard telling me that on the day we met. Walking through a crowd always reminds me of it. I move along the pavement, trailing my fingers against the shop windows. People step to the side when they get close to me. They do it without thought, without making eye contact. On the day after I died I stood in the middle of the street and screamed at the top of my voice. I cursed at people, stood in their way, threw things. The biggest reaction I got was an annoyed frown, and even that disappeared the moment they laid eyes on something else.

Leonard found me here, took me to a quiet corner of the bookstore and explained the situation. He broke the news gently, his weathered face and nicotine-scarred voice full of compassion. I still didn't take it well. I blamed him for some stupid reason and refused to speak to him for two weeks, but he forgave me. Leonard always was a good guy.

I follow three women carrying shopping bags into a

coffee shop. They ooh and ah over the pastry case, arguing about whether their shopping spree has burned enough calories to justify a brownie. I walk behind the counter, open the case, and select two sugar cookies with thick orange and black frosting. The sullen teenager working the register briefly turns toward me, but is distracted by the next customer. I wonder what he saw in that moment when he knew there was someone else behind the counter. Maybe he saw a new employee wearing one of the coffee shop's uniforms. Maybe he saw me the way I am, but his mind convinced him that I have a right to be here.

I'm curious, so I ask. 'Hey, kid. What do I look like to you?' I walk around the counter, cut to the head of the line, and look him in the eye. 'What do I look like?'

'I'll be with you in a minute, Ma'am,' he says without really looking at me. I know better. I've tried buying food the way the living do. A few times I even got someone to take my order, but they ended up giving it to someone else.

'Fuck you.' I slap the tip jar to the floor, sending quarters and dimes rolling everywhere.

'Shit.' The cashier kneels and begins sweeping up his tips. 'Sorry, Miss,' he says to the woman behind me. 'I've been really clumsy all day.'

I take my cookies and go outside, blinking fast to hold back tears. I always feel this way after I've done something cruel. All too often I do something that seems perfectly reasonable until I start thinking about what that poor teenager wants to buy with the money he makes at that crappy job. Still, even knowing how bad I'm going to feel later, I find myself doing this kind of thing more and more. I know it's not fair to hate the living but I can't help it. They're selfish. So few of them ever bother trying to see the dead, and those who do don't seem to be looking properly.

I lean against the wall of the coffee shop and watch the women with the shopping bags sit at one of the outdoor tables. One got the brownie, the other two salads. I used to be like them, worrying about my weight and my looks. Now I eat whatever the hell I want and I don't change one iota.

A middle-aged couple wanders down the pavement. The man has his arm around the woman's waist. He says something and she playfully bumps him with her shoulder. When they look at each other, they have warm, gentle smiles. I've seen this type before. These are the for life, for better or for worse, together for eternity type. I'm sure they will die within six months of each other. They'll probably be lucky enough to die in the same place, so they won't have to be alone. Or maybe they'll get to skip this haunting bullshit and go straight to whatever comes next.

Without taking my eyes off them, I reach out and claw at the wall. Three of my fingernails rip off, leaving little smears of blood on the bricks. I inhale and close my eyes, riding the pain. For the brief minute when the pain is at its most intense, the loneliness is gone. The nerve endings in my fingers feel like they're on fire, and

I have to lean on the wall to keep from passing out, but I still smile through the tears. Then I watch as my fingernails grow back and the blood on the wall turns to vapour. I feel a bit sleepy, dreamy. The lonely ache in my chest will return, but for now it is dull and easy to ignore.

I leave my place against the wall and wander into another shop, this one a thrift store specialising in funky retro clothes. I strip right there in the middle of the store and put on a white ball gown that probably sat in someone's closet for sixty years before it got here. I twirl and pirouette between the racks of clothes, adding combat boots and a top hat to my ensemble. I laugh at how I look in the mirror and decide that a cigar is just the touch my outfit needs.

There aren't any cigars sold on my little street, though. I should know. I could probably recite the entire inventory of half the stores here. No cigars, but the bookstore sells a lot of interesting stuff. Maybe I'll find something there.

I may spend a lot of time yelling at God and calling him a sick fuck, but I do send up a little thank you every time I think about how of all the streets in Phoenix to be stuck on, I got one with a great big bookstore. When I come here and curl up in a chair with a book, I almost feel normal again. To my delight, I see a copy of the latest book by my favorite author. I open it, bury my face in the pages, and breathe in the smell. My hat and boots suddenly make me feel silly, so I leave them on the discount table.

I used to do things like that to get noticed. Leonard told me early on it wouldn't do any good, but I kept making messes and rearranging things and scribbling messages on walls. I tried picking up objects and waving them around, thinking it would be like in movies, that they would see whatever I was holding magically suspended in the air. Everything I did was blamed on someone else. I even went out on the street and punched a guy in the face, but he just turned around and started fighting with the man next to him. Leonard got mad at me for that.

'Listen, girl. We occupy a blind spot. So do our actions,' Leonard told me, struggling to keep his voice calm. 'The living will do just about anything to convince themselves we're not here. So stop taking it out on people because it won't do any good.'

I walk upstairs, find a comfortable chair and survey the crowd. I realise this is the first time I've been on the store's upper floor since Leonard left. He and I used to sit here and watch people for hours. Those were almost good times, when Leonard and I had each other for companionship. It's funny; he and I never would have spoken to each other while alive, but as ghosts we were best friends for years. I guess Mr. Twain was right when he wrote that death is a great leveller.

Leonard told me he died of heat stroke. It was one of the hottest days in Arizona history. He was in his usual spot, begging for change, when it killed him. This occurred around his 60th birthday, ending a life in which he started and lost several businesses, married four times, fathered six children, set foot on every continent except Antarctica, and ended up on the streets when the bottle got the better of him.

Leonard told that story on my second day as a dead woman. I envied him, in a way. I wanted a story like that. Mine is so banal it's hardly worth mentioning. My mother and I were shoe shopping when a blood vessel burst in my brain. It was a ridiculous congenital defect that could have killed me at any point in my life, but chose to do it at that precise moment, barely a month after I turned twenty-two.

'Don't be a fool, girl,' Leonard said when I told him how I felt. 'You'll look young and healthy and pretty for eternity. I look like shoe leather.'

It was in this place Leonard told me he was leaving. 'What do you mean?' I asked. In the seven years since I died, neither of us had ever been able to leave this street, this little strip of the city. We never figured out why. All we knew was that there may as well have been a brick wall any time we tried to step over a certain line. I tried to leap through the barrier once, but it knocked me on my arse like I'd grabbed an electric fence.

Leonard rubbed his scraggly beard and frowned. 'I don't know. I just get this feeling I'll be leaving soon.'

'You mean...' I made some vague gesture. Neither Leonard nor I could bring ourselves to say something as corny as 'crossing over' or 'moving on'.

He nodded.

'No,' I whispered. 'Oh, no, no, Leonard, you can't.'

'Not sure I'll have much of a choice, girl,' he replied mildly.

'Leonard, you can't leave me alone.'

My friend sipped his coffee and stared into space for several moments. 'I don't know how this works. I was alone for a year before you came along. Maybe you'll leave at the same time as me, maybe you'll be here another fifty years.' He gave me a tired smile. 'Someone's bound to die on this street sometime. Anyway, you're strong. You'll survive it. Hell, you're already dead, how could you not survive it?'

But I almost didn't. The next day Leonard was gone. No bright light, no heavenly choir, just there one day and gone the next. There's a lot of that year I don't remember. I have a few hazy images of slicing at my wrists, the pavement speeding closer as I jumped off a rooftop, the headlights of a car just before it crashed into me. None of it worked, of course.

I'm sitting and thinking about that terrible year when I hear music over the sounds of the customers. I stand and go downstairs, straining to hear where the music is coming from. It gets louder for a second when someone opens the glass door. Following the sound, I go outside and walk down to the corner.

A young man sits on a folding chair and plays a guitar. The guitar case sits open in front of him, a few coins and dollar bills inside. He is around the age I was when I died, with curly dark hair and kind eyes. His fingers move effortlessly over the strings while he sings with a strong, clear voice. It's a song I recognise, a sad Irish folk song about a woman at a well. Two old people pause, listen, and toss some money into the guitar case. He

146

gives them a nod of gratitude without interrupting the music.

When that song is over, he moves seamlessly into a catchy pub song. I smile and begin tapping my feet, swaying just a little to the tune. Two women walk by while yammering into their mobile phones. Furious, I dip my hand into one of their purses and pull out a wallet. I find over two hundred dollars in cash, all of which I place in the guitar case.

I stand there for nearly two hours. The guitar player pauses once in a while to drink some water or think about what to play next. I keep waiting for him to find the two hundred dollars. I want to see the surprise and delight on his face. But he doesn't even seem to see the money. He never looks at it or stops to count it.

He is in the middle of a fast-paced jig. A crowd of four or five people has gathered to listen. He finishes the jig to some scattered clapping and applause. At that moment he lifts his head, looks directly into my eyes, and smiles. Then, without looking away, he begins playing a slow, soulful ballad.

He is smiling at me. He is playing me a song. For the first time in ten years, I exist to a living person. I stand rooted to the spot, terrified that the slightest movement will destroy this moment. Several times his eyes move toward his guitar, but always come back to me. All the background noise fades to nothing; I can't hear anything but this song.

It ends too soon. The last chord dies away, and he looks around, confused. He is trying to catch sight of that girl who was watching him so intently, that pale girl with the deep brown eyes and the white dress. I want to tell him that I'm still here, I'm still right in front of him, but it will break my heart if I speak to him and he doesn't hear me.

He begins packing up, expression troubled. He scoops the money out of the case and stuffs it into his pocket without counting it. The guitar he treats with respect, placing it carefully in the case, making sure the lid is secure. Lifting the case in his right hand and the folding chair under his arm, he walks off down the street. I follow a step or two behind. He has a nice walk, a relaxed, casual amble. His head turns occasionally; he likes watching his surroundings. I want to know his name.

We draw close to the line I can't cross. I move desperately forward, standing so he and I are chest to chest. He walks around me like I'm a trashcan or a phone booth. He heads for the crosswalk. I begin to panic as I imagine what it will be like if he never comes back, if he never visits this street and never plays me another song. My teeth bite into my lip until blood trickles down my chin.

I see a car coming toward us. It will pass us in a few seconds. Standing right behind him, I whisper, 'Please.'

He hears me. He starts to turn. With all my strength, I push him. As he falls, I snatch the guitar case out of his hand. I hear the screech of brakes and smell rubber from the tyres. I don't watch him die. It's not important how it happens, whether he is crushed beneath the wheels or if his neck breaks on impact or if his skull cracks on the pavement. It's not important how the people around me try to save him by performing CPR and calling an ambulance. What is important is that when he leaves his body, I will be standing here holding his guitar, waiting for him.

Dawn

Morag Edward

'Eat your breakfast, darling,' says my mummy. I am stirring the cornflakes with my spoon, washing big waves over soggy islands and flicking flakes out of the milky ocean. I'm not hungry.

Breakfast isn't as good as usual.

'Aren't you hungry pet? Come on, you've got to finish it.' I scoop the breakfast into heaps and shovel it into my mouth, dribbling milk down my chin. I want to go back to bed, but after last night want just as much to stay awake.

I make the mistake of writing about the night visitor in my weekend diary jotter in class. Mrs Dunmore wants to hear more at playtime and so I tell her all about it, specially how scary the shadow man is and how I can't move at all, not even to scream, then I get to go out to play. After playtime my parents arrive at school and we go in a small room with other grown-ups and the headmistress. I have to draw pictures of monsters and I do the ones from Doctor Who because I've never seen any for real, but the teacher seems to like them, and also pictures of my house and my family. I make those up because I am bored and I don't know what our roof really looks like but it should have a chimney with smoke so I add one. Then I have to tell stories about the pictures and the grown-ups ask me hundreds and hundreds of questions about the stories and the chimney. After that I have to play with two dolls - a girl doll and a boy doll - and they have all the bits like people, not dolls, which is really embarrassing and every time I make them pretend to talk to each other all the grown-ups look at each other and write in their jotters.

I don't know why they're not listening properly but they are all like they're a bit deaf or they think I'm really stupid. I keep saying I don't know the dark man, and maybe he is just a bad dream, and no, he's never touched me, and that just makes them all look at each other again and now my mummy is crying again, which is embarrassing and daddy is starting to shout at all the other grown-ups and he makes my teacher cry too which is really weird because teachers don't cry. I am glad when it is time to go home, but am thinking that I am in trouble for something and there will be an atmosphere.

But the grown-ups stay in the room for ages more and I sit in the other with a fat lady who stares too much and says she's a psychologist so understands me whenever I say anything, but I only want to go to the toilet.

When we go home mummy and daddy talk about the weather and holidays and food. When my brother complains about his late teatime and asks what I've done wrong now they shush him and say that I have a very good imagination and might write books when I am grown up, isn't that nice. My brother thinks that's silly, can we have chips as a treat.

The next time any teacher asks us to write about the weekends in our diary jotter I just write about my budgie and how he likes to eat chips too.

I wake at dawn, shivering and sweating. I remember this feeling. I don't want to open my eyes but I have to; I know it has returned. The shape is sitting on the end of the bed, half turned away from me, the face in shadow. It isn't looking towards me, but seems to be staring at the floor. My eyes are burning with fatigue, brain switching off already, pulling me, dragging me down into sleep, my eyelids fluttering as I slip back into sleep. As my eyes close I see the head turn towards me. I wouldn't have thought it was possible to fall asleep through a thick fog of terror, but it is. It's like drowning.

The next night I wake as though someone has shaken me from a deep sleep. The shock and confusion take a few seconds to wear off sufficiently to realise I am briefly and partially awake, in my bed, in my room. And that I'm not alone. The figure is sitting on my bed, but not at the end of the bed. He is sitting at my feet. Every muscle, nerve and terrified thought of escape screams to stay awake but they lose the battle to the chemicals of sleep numbing me, dragging me down into oblivion. As my eyelids flicker shut, the head turns to look at me.

This happens almost every week now. I always think it'll stop or that I'll get used to the disrupted sleep, or maybe I'll break free from the sleep paralysis and fight it and make it leave, but then it happens again the same as before.

I don't dare tell anyone, no matter how scared I am or how sick I feel in the morning. I know perfectly well what the adults will suspect of these teenage ramblings: lies, abuse or insanity, same as when I was little. Instead I stay awake as far into the night as I can, window locked, chair against the door; staring at the ceiling until the first light of dawn begins to change the colour of the curtains. I usually manage to get about two hours of sleep before the alarm goes off for school, but at least the sleep is undisturbed until then. I catch up on the missed sleep in class.

I must have fallen asleep shortly after lying down that night. I don't know what time it is when I slam into consciousness, but the house is silent and dark. My breathing isn't quite under my control yet, body still more asleep than awake, and it is through half-open eyes and a vague mental haze that I register my surroundings. And see the figure sitting on the bed, head bowed away from me. It is sitting by my legs.

I examine the bruise on the side of my knee in the morning, a faint purplish mark. I can't remember having hit it against anything, but it's still sore. The bruise fades fast but that ache lingers.

It is almost a year later when I burst out of peaceful sleep into half-waking panic and know it is in my room with me again before I even open my eyes. I have to open my eyes though, have to look. It is sitting by my hips. So close I think I can hear it breathing.

Pulling on my pants in the morning I notice a small bruise on my hipbone. I'm not sure why but I immediately check the other side. There is another bruise on that hipbone too. And more bruises on my legs. I dress as fast as possible so that I can open the curtains and flood the room with sunlight.

Winter comes. I go to sleep curled up small against the far side of the bed pressed right up against the wall but I wake up on my back, arms by my side. It is sitting beside me. So close it is hard to breathe, in case I brush against it. As I fall back into the panicked sleep I think it leans towards me. Over me.

When my alarm clock rings it takes me a while to be able to wake enough to reach out to hit the off button. My chest feels wheezy and heavy, ribs hurting from the inside. It has been a struggle to move my arms at all, as though every muscle is injured and weak. I think I see a bruise on my ribs as I shower, but it might have been the shadow from my breast. There aren't any other visible injuries at all this time.

Time passes. I can't remember life being any other way.

The first time I have sex it is in the hills in the afternoon so that doesn't count, but the first time my boyfriend and I do it indoors we fall asleep in his bed afterwards. I doze off, so relaxed and warm that I am happy enough to let sleep happen. Almost. I suddenly remember what else sleep brings, and don't know what on earth to do, already starting to ease away from the now snoring lump by my side. But as I try to move away he wraps his arms right around me and squeezes me tight, in his sleep, and I am so amazed at this unconscious protectiveness or whatever it is, that I risk settling down with him. I risk sleeping with him.

Almost seven months of nights with Michael and the dark figure never shows up, not once. I often still leap awake, hearing a noise or imagining things in my dreams, but the room is always empty, just me and my boyfriend. I think he might be surprised that he's been made so welcome at my flat so fast, but I don't want to be alone in the dark anymore. But we are young and we fight about stupid things, and I get so fed up with him that he leaves me and I finally go to sleep alone. When I wake at dawn the room is dimly lit by the street lamp's sodium glow. I am frozen in half-sleep but my eyes are open and I can see the dark figure is on my bed, leaning towards me.

In the shower the next morning I see the three small cuts across my ribs and one on my neck. I clean them up, get dried and dressed, and phone Michael to ask him to come back, to move in properly and permanently.

I love being married, cuddling up to someone to spend the night safe and warm. The fear of sleep eventually fades, and I store memories of those bad nights with all the other nightmares, regrets and doubts. If I wake now the only thing in my bedroom is my husband, and that is the way it should be. There is nothing in the shadows, nothing on the end of the bed, nothing in the room at all. I feel as though I've escaped into a better place than I used to belong to. As long as Michael's arms are around me, nothing comes near me at night, in sleep, dreams or wakefulness.

I don't know when it all changes. He still seems happy and we have life together pretty well sorted out now. But I'm beginning to feel as though I have become my own husband's mistress, an addition to his life. I know he hasn't been unfaithful, but whatever is his main partner, it isn't me. I don't know if it is his work, his mates, his past, his hobbies or even just himself, but they are what he is really married to and he isn't sharing. When he finishes whatever he is doing, he comes home to me, we have fun, we are in love, and after a while of enjoying being with me I can see that he's looking forward to getting back to the rest of it. Half of his mind is already out there, but any attempt to draw him in and question it is denied with such fervour that it would seem that he at least believes what he is saying. But loved as I am, I know I'm not nearly his most favourite thing, and that sort of downsizing eats away at a person's morale and self-esteem. I married to share life, not be an extra. We bicker, restlessly. By the end of the year he has gone altogether.

It is hard to sleep alone. The novelty of clean fresh sheets and a peaceful bed to stretch out in soon wears off and the room just feels empty. I turn to say something, share something, move closer for warmth and then realise

I don't have anyone, that it is just me now. I tried to remind myself it was like that even when he was living with me, but my mind is already making him seem more of a partner than he actually was, and I feel the loneliness as though it is something new. Sometimes I think I feel his arms around me as I fall asleep, but when I wake I remember and realise.

It takes a few months before I grow accustomed to the silence, but I'm not as calm as I had been with him. I don't think I'll ever get used to the emptiness at night.

I wake with a jump in the darkness. It is a huge shock to the system to go from peaceful sleep to full alertness and my skin bristles and sweats and my heart pounds as though trying to escape from my ribcage again. It will only be a brief break from sleep though; as soon as I am awake I am already starting to fall asleep again, dragged back down as though drugged. My eyelids are still open but my body is still immobilised by sleep hormones; comatose, breathing audible and on automatic, heart-rate slowing down. It is through this that I vaguely focus on the shape in the room, the figure that is sitting on the bed by my side. It is half turned away from me, the face in shadow, silhouetted against the faint glow of the curtains. It isn't looking towards me, but seems to be staring at the floor.

My heart races faster and hammers harder, breath failing to catch up, eyes burning with the effort of keeping them open. But my treacherous brain is switching off in the background, trying to drag me back down into unconsciousness. As my eyes start flicker closed I see the shadowed head turn towards me, and then lean down right over me, blocking out the dawn.

So I reach out to it.

The Devil's Tavern

Alison J. Littlewood

Jeering rose from the street outside the tavern. It was always the same on such a day. Jack knew how it felt, the pushing and jostling, the stares of hatred from strangers and old acquaintances alike. Some would throw things, eggs that had gone rotten, or cabbages. 'Don't worry,' they'd shout. 'The Thames'll wash you clean.'

It washed away sins, too, that's what they said, although a heavy, brown kind of clean it must be from such a river. The kind of clean Jack Flanagan felt.

There was a clatter of footsteps on the jetty stair outside. Then silence. The lashing had begun.

Jack stared into the empty grate, but the scene was replayed before his eyes. He knew how it felt – being dragged down to the waterline, feet sinking deep into cold silt. The hands on his arms, pulling them around the posts that supported what had come to be known as the Devil's Tavern.

They would be winding thick ropes around Tom Makinson now, wrapping them over the cross beams to prevent him shinning up the post to save his life.

Jack wondered if he was struggling, or weeping, or whether he had walked to his death with his head held high. Whether, given the chance, he would change places with someone else. One life for another. As he had.

Final shouts were heard from the riverbank. And Tom Makinson, Jack's friend and partner, began the slow wait for the water to rise and rob him of his breath.

High tide brought death in its heavy swell; low tide brought the gulls, to bury their beaks in overblown flesh and peck at tender eyes. But it would be three days before they cut Tom down, bloated and swollen, to be buried at last in the solid earth. Until then he would be a warning to those who passed down the river – smugglers, press gangs, thieves, and all who frequented the Devil's Tavern and gave it its name.

Little wonder then, that Jack could hear his unfortunate friend, the once jocular tones raised in anger and in fear.

'Damn you all to hell,' it said. And then: 'I'll be seeing you, Jack Flanagan!'

Jack could no more stay away from the tavern than his friend could escape its shadow. All night he had turned, troubled by the thought of him, haunted by the easy trust they had placed in each other.

Flagons of ale and easy laughter had shaped their plan, along with the sweet taste of bootleg rum. Tom would buy barrel-loads of it from the Indes, hide it behind a cargo of dyewoods, and bring it to the tavern. Then into Jack's hold it would go, and on up to Hull.

'Their customs are slovens compared to the City men,' Tom had said, slurring his words and throwing an arm around Jack. 'A fortune, lad. It'll make us a small fortune.'

Tom's rum. Tom's delivery. Tom's idea. Jack's role had been nothing, or so he told himself.

And now the river would claim his friend, rising inch by inch as light faded from the sky until it covered Tom's feet, his breeches, his chest: reaching his mouth, his nose, and then his eyes. Leaving him in darkness while the Thames continued its steady course.

Jack dressed slowly, his back troubled by the flogging he had received in place of death. They'd used the cat, a whip with nine knotted strings that drew blood where they landed. Then they'd pressed gunpowder into the wounds. It had been like fire, like hell. The scars were blackened, a wavering tattoo that pictured nothing.

At the tavern he stared into his ale as the Thames softly began to recede once more.

Then a cry roused Jack from his reverie.

'What in God's name was that?'

A portly man with a beard red as a fox scraped back his chair. He waved his arm about, motioning for silence, and gradually the bar grew still.

Then Jack heard it. A low, rasping moan, coming from beneath his feet.

'I'll see you there...'

The man with the red hair crossed himself.

'...Coming for you. I'm coming for you...'

Jack froze while around him men rose to their feet, rushed to the windows, or shouted and crossed themselves by turns. At last, the red-haired sailor headed for the stair.

'Someone's having a little joke on us, lads,' he said. 'But I'm going down anyway. Let's show 'em the colour of our mettle, eh?'

A few 'Ayes' were heard, and the men headed for the river. After a moment, Jack followed.

The men held the tavern's supports as they stepped onto the treacherous silt. Jack's view was blocked by those who went before him, but he could hear their gasps of wonder and of fear.

'What the...'

'Impossible.'

'It's a trick, some trick.'

He pressed his way between them, and when the other men saw that he had come, they drew aside to let him pass.

His friend hung there, head drooping onto his chest. His hair hung dark and slick across his pale forehead. His whole body sagged, held in place only by the ropes that bound him.

Then, slowly, he raised his head and stared straight at Jack. His once clear blue eyes were pale and watery, but all the same, a fire seemed to burn inside them.

'Two days, Jack,' he said. 'Two more. And then I'm coming for you.'

Redditch Library
Tel: 01905 822722

Loans summary

Library Card ID: ****6006
Date: 17/02/2022   11:00

Loaned today

Title: The arrivals
Due back: 10/03/2022

Title: The war of the poor
Due back: 10/03/2022

Title: Grunt : the curious science…
Due back: 10/03/2022

Title: A life in nature, or, How to…
Due back: 10/03/2022

Title: Read by dawn. Vol. 3
Due back: 10/03/2022

Total item(s) loaned today: 5
Outstanding charges 0 80 GBP
Overdue: 0
Reservation(s) to collect: 0
Total item(s) on loan: 5

www.worcestershire.gov.uk/libraries

They watched from the deck of a lighter, Jack sitting apart from the others, waiting to see who would cut Tom Makinson loose for the night. Perhaps they would give him a hollow pipe to breathe through, or carry out some other trick. But none had come. There was only a soft breeze on the water, moonlight shining on the brown swell, and the distant sound of the docks that were never still.

As daylight broadened and the waters began to fall once more, the watchers sat straighter, rubbing their bleary eyes. And slowly, Tom's body was revealed.

His face was pale and swollen, as though he was blowing out his cheeks, and it had turned the greyish blue of the sea on a cloudy day. There was a wound on his cheek. It looked as if something had been feeding there.

When he turned to face the watching men they could see how his eyes bulged. The light within them was crazed now, and shone brighter than ever.

'One more, Jack,' he said. 'One more.'

But the next day, Tom Makinson was dead.

They cut him down, his body flopping heavily onto the silt. Water seeped from him, running from his mouth and ears and nose, back to the river. His shirt bulged where his body had swollen. His breeches were tight to his bloated legs.

His eyes were open, almost white, and soft like half-set eggs. One man tried to push his eyelids closed, but drew back when his fingers sank into the ooze. Tom's face was purple and covered with blotches and sores. Dark slime mingled with his hair.

And the stench. It rose like marsh gas, clogging the nostrils and making Jack's eyes water. It stank of rot, of death, and of the Thames.

'He'll not be coming for you now, lad,' said one of the men who stood watching.

But Jack felt no relief. He could only stare at the thing his friend had become.

That night, Jack tossed and turned like waves on the open sea. When he closed his eyes, he could see Tom still; his mind gave him no respite. It seemed that he was to provide his own punishment.

He remembered the way the customs lighter had drawn alongside, before he'd even left the Thames. The day was clear and cold, the sea a fresh, blue line in the distance. He could smell it, the salt and spray, all the time they searched his boat. How he'd cursed Tom then. Now, he would do anything to have him back. Not those cold, blank eyes, the thing he had become.

He turned again, trying to find comfort, and that was when he heard a foot on the stair. His landlord perhaps, returning to the rooms downstairs after some unaccustomed revelry.

Then he heard a dragging, sucking sound, and another footstep. Jack sat up, listening. After a moment, it came again. A footstep accompanied by a low squelch, as though someone were walking through mud. And another. Jack froze, although he could feel his heart thudding, the heat of it bursting in his chest.

The footsteps ceased outside his door. There was a pause. And then, ringing out into the night, came a loud knock.

Jack felt the hairs rise on the back of his neck as a sweet, rotten scent crept under the door.

Then the knock again. And with it, a voice.

'Do you not hear me, Jack?'

It was muffled, as though the tongue was swollen in his friend's mouth. And Jack could see him as though the door stood wide open, his globular eyes, the white, distended cheeks, seeping with sores and running with water.

'I was coming for you, Jack. But the tide...'

There was a pause, and a gulping, bubbling sob. 'I waited for you. But the last time, the tide, the river, it washed it all away. I couldn't hate any longer. I couldn't fear. I couldn't breathe...'

He paused.

'Is your soul washed clean, Jack?'

And the tears came, Jack's eyes running freely. He rose to his feet, went to the door, and turned the key. After a moment, he opened the door.

Tom stood there, still sodden with river water, his hair plastered to his skull. His shirt gaped over a purpled chest, the skin tight and glistening, as though it would split. The stench of him was worse now, like being buried in rotten eggs, in filth, in the sweet-sour smell of the river.

'It's a cold death, Jack,' he whispered. 'A cold death. God help me, but if I could have given you up...'

His eyes were pale and watery, but no light shone there. They were flat and clean as paper.

'I'm sorry,' said Jack, and covered his eyes.

Then he felt something on his shoulder, the light touch of a hand. And he raised his eyes to see his friend turning, to leave him standing there.

'Wait,' said Jack.

He followed him down the stair, Tom's progress slow and cumbersome, and out into the street. It was quiet and lit only by moonlight. They made their way across the cobbles, Tom's steps tentative and gentle, as though he feared his flesh would not last the journey.

Down the hill they went, the two friends who had shared ale, coin, song and laughter, all under the eaves of the Devil's Tavern. One marked now by fire, the other by water. They did not speak, and they did not look back.

They only walked, arm in arm, towards the cold of the waiting Thames.

Tinsel

Frazer Lee

Tom's breath fogged up his window then disappeared like a ghost. He tried again, but no luck – the frost clinging to the outside of the windowpane refused to melt. He wished his parents would just go to bed. He'd been kneeling here on his bed, leaning on the windowsill for what seemed like an eternity. Then – footsteps on the stairs. Action stations.

It was Mum, here to tuck Tom into bed. He lay rigidly still, breathing heavily with his arms by his side. He felt his mother's shadow falling over him as she leaned in to kiss him softly on the head. Then she grabbed him and tickled him. He let out a loud giggle. How on earth did she do that every time? Anyone else would've fallen for it and believed he was asleep, but not Mum with her amazing radar skills.

They shared a laugh about it and she kissed him again and turned off the light. He listened intently as Mum closed the door and went back downstairs to the living room. *'Must be wrapping my presents right now,'* he thought, his ears conjuring sounds of foil paper and sticky tape.

This was the most crucial part of Christmas Eve for Tom – waiting for Mum, Dad and Big Sis to come to bed. Then he had to leave it for just long enough to make sure they were asleep, without nodding off himself and missing his chance. Still listening intently, he remembered how he'd bungled the job two years ago, when he was just eight. He was older now, and wiser – an expert in nocturnal manoeuvres. One day he'd be a secret agent...

Tom awoke with a jolt and shivered. His bedclothes had made a bid for freedom, leaving just his pyjamas to protect him. He grabbed his alarm clock, the luminous face teasing him with the time. Four o'clock a.m. Oh, flipping brilliant, he'd nodded off and been asleep for hours. But there was still time. He'd better move fast and silent, like that amazing ninja he'd seen on the telly.

He swung his legs over the side of the bed, and ever so carefully stood up. Without a sound, he crept over to the door and removed his dressing gown from the door handle. Tom loved his dressing gown – it was fleecy and so cosy, especially good for a nippy night like this. Careful now, this was where it could all go horribly wrong. One false move and he'd wake the whole household. He reached out for the door handle, his arm rehearsing the exact distance he could open the door before it creaked. Slowly, slowly, he pulled the door open, slipped sideways through the gap, grabbed the outside handle and closed the door behind him with the tiniest click.

Heart beating, Tom stood on the dark landing for a

few seconds, catching his breath. That was intense, his best ninja move ever. Satisfied he hadn't woken his folks, he padded gently across the landing towards the stairs. The soft, soundless carpet beneath his feet, he allowed his mind to wander a little. He began thinking of the prize that awaited him at the end of his mission, remembering how wonderful his presents had looked under the tree last year. They'd gleamed in their shiny wrapping paper like treasure, begging him to squeeze them. He'd picked up the biggest first, giving it a gentle rock to hear and feel what was inside. It didn't take a genius to realise it was the games console he'd wanted. The box had matched the dimensions of the one in the shop exactly – he should know, he'd examined the display case at the supermarket enough times while Mum spent an age at the deli counter. Tom felt a rush of panic. Had he dropped enough hints about the music player? Maybe she hadn't noticed during her massive quest for breaded products and two-for-one deals on the way to the checkout. Maybe he hadn't been clear enough about the colour of the headphones – oh no, what a disaster. His pace quickened as he reached the foot of the stairs.

An animal hiss erupted in his ears as he stepped into the hallway. Tom searched the gloom for the source of the din, dropping to his knees to peer under the sideboard. Wild eyes suddenly glared at him from the shadows there, along with more violent hissing. It was Fudge, the family cat. Whispering as loud as he dared, Tom told Fudge to be quiet. The animal shrank back beneath the sideboard with a final exasperated meow. The cat had almost been his undoing, but failure was not an option. He had to go and squeeze and prod at all the parcels bearing his name.

Downstairs was even chillier than his bedroom, cold seeping into the hallway through hidden nooks and crannies. Tom pulled his dressing gown tighter and snuck into the living room. It was pitch black inside, owing to Mum's annoying habit of switching everything off and unplugging it every night, 'to be on the safe side.' This often drove Dad to distraction; especially if he'd set the tellybox to record late night sports shows. An acrid metallic smell filled the room. What had they been wrapping in here? *'Only one way to find out,'* thought Tom as he edged his way around the perimeter of the room, feeling along the cabinet, then the wall. Finally, he felt the Christmas tree as he brushed against it. Baubles clinked icily as he located the power cord and followed it, crawling across the floor to the power socket in the corner. He felt the cold metal pins in his hand and turning the plug right side up, inserted it into the wall. Something wet dripped on his hand just as he pressed the switch. Something heavy and slick slid across his head.

Tom scrabbled backwards in shock. Looking up, he saw the fairy lights twinkling. But they were red, not clear, as they had been earlier today and all last week since they'd decorated the tree. He stared, mouth agape, as he realised the lights weren't red after all. Rather, it was what hung around them that gave them their crimson glow.

The Christmas tree was slicked with blood and covered

in strands of flesh and hair. Mum's hair, and his sister's. He could pick out his Dad's tattoo on a piece of bloodied skin that dangled above a bauble like a handkerchief. Drooping branches struggled beneath the weight of the innards scattered across them like red tinsel. Ruined organs steamed like butcher's offal at the hot kiss of the lights. Eyeballs hung there like baubles. He could recognise some of the pieces – he'd seen them in the big pop-up anatomy book at school – a section of intestine here, a tangle of veins there.

Tom scrambled to his feet. Nausea hit him and he vomited stomach bile onto the living room rug. Turning fearfully around, he saw his family lying lifeless on the sofa like grotesque dolls. Their bodies had been torn apart. Flesh ravaged and ribcages exposed like the hulls of broken ships.

The room span, and Tom sank to his knees, a dry scream dying in his throat.

Then, he saw them.

Cold eyes, watching him from the dark black of the fireplace. Watching him touching his presents.

Sighs

Patricia MacCormack

She opened her eyes and smelled heady smells of field mice and hares. Little smells of little bloodied bodies. She rolled the odour over the back of her tongue and swallowed it. Its warmth was the warmth of bruising. A florid bruise blossomed over her chest. Contusion and she desired something. Blind. The sun burned her eyes and she longed for the sisterhood of darkness, or at least a soothing myopia. She fantasised life below where she lay. Industrious life of armoured little creatures. Not warm, baying mammals but insects, hard bodied, without artery or vein. The thought of their rushing metropolis surrounding her left her cold and raw. She breathed deeply for the warm smell of insignificant, vulnerable animal. Animals that *felt*. Felt pain, felt warmth. Animals with autonomy and desire and fear. Animals that wanted to be alive, that *emitted*. Her ear was so close to the dirt she thought she could hear whispers and moans. Beneath her the earth became agitated, bumped and pushed upward.

Fingers, there were fingers under her back, shrouded

in a flimsy glove of soil. Reaching for her, trying to reach *in* her. The flesh clothing her back tore, broke open and the bony tendrils of the beings beneath entered her. They were trying to pull something from her. She could smell what they wanted. She did not scream. She could not weep, for there was no real pain or fear. Her eyes rolled impossibly backwards, like a frightened calf, so that only the whites were exposed to the scalding sun. She arched her spine upward, bringing with it the fingers which were now clutched around her respective ribs. Arched as if frozen in a coital state, she sighed.

Lara hated her lungs. The two flesh sponges in her frail chest had let her down so many times that by the time she was nineteen she knew it would be their failure which would eventually take her life. She just hoped that it would be lung decomposition at a ripe age over premature collapse of the respiratory system just when she had grown up enough to live a little. She huffed in another coveted gush of air and drank it desperately. She lay on her back in her bed, counting the cobwebs hanging from the architrave above her, feeling like the air she sucked deeply brought with it the filmy trails of web she watched float in their ocean of breeze. Once in her chest they would wrap around her bronchial tubes and lovingly squeeze and squeeze. And as her breast-bone sank in her breath would only reach her throat, becoming tighter with asphyxiation until her mouth alone would fill with oxygen. But that would be useless. Lara heaved in another wheezy lung full. She would die of it, perhaps, but there was no real need to fantasise it first. Her sister told her repeatedly that morbidity enhanced all illness. Her sister Claudia, who also delighted in calling her a hypochondriac, even when Lara sat in casualty with a nebuliser mask plastered to her face.

It was no wonder Lara had a lung obsession. She exhaled a loud whistle of air as a fine tendril of spun web settled over her brow. An image clouded her eyes. Ectoplasmic hands around her neck, thumbs caving in her larynx. Palms pressing her sternum in some insane version of CPR. These were real hands she felt. The sensation was simply too strong to be internally automated. And why the hell would her body want to suffocate itself? The body and its little jokes on man, Lara mused. She would have almost smirked if her mouth had not been occupied with a grimace of constriction. More webs fell, more death-rattle breaths writhed their way into Lara's maze of lung. Each and every breath Lara inhaled seemed to tease her, promising it would reach her alveoli, but never really offering her satiation. She ran her dry tongue along the roof of her sticky mouth and arched her throat forward. It made a creaking noise as she whistled in one more breath. Her sister, in her academic virtue, had given Lara a book. Lara lay in bed, contorted in breathlessness, and the tome had been flung onto the coverlet as recognition that Lara was indeed sick, ('though you do play it up, you self-pitying drama queen'). Claudia had decided it was as morbidly driven and obsessive as Lara. One of Claudia's cynical maxims was that sympathetic was the same without the 'sym', and people who practised sympathy were as simpering as those who welcomed it. Lara was satisfied enough with the bizarre libation without needing florid articulation to go with it.

The essay was, thought Lara, written by a maudlin paranoiac on some uniquely Victorian drug. She would have loved the opinion of any one of her retentive professors of this particular 'classic'. The cover of the book was an abstract nightmare. No title, just an amorphic swirl of what were perhaps emergent creatures, andromorphs and voluminous darknesses. The sensation of the metallic ridges and puffed hide in her nostrils and around her taste-buds gave her immense pleasure. It smelled like dustblown pig. Against her tongue it felt like flesh. A whistling exhalation climaxed the experience.

Suspiria de Profundis, the title page stated. Lara was classically educated enough to translate it as 'Sighs from the Depths', and ignorant enough to be thankful that the title was the only Latin of the book. Apparently the book was something of a sequel by a self-proclaimed opium-eater (opium gorger, thought Lara). Thomas De Quincey was an essayist who received little attention in anthologies of English literature she used for English 101, (the volumes of which made the bible look like a pocket-reader).Considering her aversion to the hideously overlong tomes of Norton, it was probably in De Quincey's favour that he was absent.

His writings were not inaccessible, though often obscure. One essay in particular Lara drank into her lungs more deeply and easily than she could ever drink air. She respirated what it told her and felt its ideas and images oxygenate her blood. If De Quincey was an opium eater, then she was an eater of his words. She ate of his brain and the taste was satisfyingly nutritious. This essay spoke of women, symbols of ascendance, tears, darkness and sighs. This essay, 'Levana and Our Ladies of Sorrow'. Levana who raises aloft; The Mother of Tears which mourn; Darkness, defier of God. Darkness and tears were, thought Lara, clichés in this jaded landscape. The one banally prevalent, the other materially tangible and too signifying. Darkness and tears were obviously undesirable conclusions. Abstract, perhaps, but hardly enigmatic or fresh. They were even something to be blasé about. They are familiar, comfortable fears.

But neither material nor conceptual and both. Suspiria? *Sighs*?

From reading De Quincey, Lara was repetitiously confronted and obsessed by the desire for intimate knowledge of what the opium-eater meant by sighs. A sigh is a sigh. It's really a nothing, an overly loud exhalation. Lara lived with respiration like that. Almost every one of her breaths was a sigh of a sort. Surely in making a trinity of misery, of evil, De Quincey could have thought of something far more obviously congruent with darkness and tears. Man's heart incarnated its suffering as many more explicit entities; despair, torment, trauma, rage, guilt, even death. Sighing was an ethereal nothing. And in its ethereality it certainly didn't lend itself well to being made physically incarnate. Tears and darkness you could touch, you could take. And you could create.

Lara sat in her window seat, staring at the pitch sky,

her thoughts rolling turbulently, mirroring the grey clouds which rolled over the night in a threatening tide. Working something out, but never really coming to a conclusion. Just rolling over and over, growing more shrouded, darker. Their tide rolled in but it never left anything on the shore of her mind as they retreated. Lara felt her throat constricted by a winding sheet of frustration. She was lucid, intellectually dexterous to the point of precociousness. Why did this concept so elude her? She scratched her neck and exhaled loudly. But the itch didn't go away. Lara dug her fingernails into her neck and dragged them across the irritation. It wasn't really like an itch though. It felt more deliberate, more specific. It felt like there was something in her neck, pushing at the skin. She wrenched her hand away and looked at it. After she was sufficiently repelled by the skin and blood under her fingernails her eyes travelled down to her palm. It was there as well. Tiny bumps rippling along her hand, leaving trails of contusion. She grimaced in disgust. Ordinarily Lara would have thought she was hallucinating, but there was something deliciously indicative in these stigmata. Was this her flesh incarnating her frustration? The autonomy her body was illustrating horrified her. Frightening her concept of will. And God, it hurt. But what would hurt more was if it ceased. It was giving her something, or working something out for her.

Suddenly she was compulsed. There were fingers running down the inside of her neck, teasing her tendons like a violin and she knew what to do. She went to the kitchen, to the block of laser knives (laser because they never need sharpening...never) and chose the tiny fish-boning knife. It was pliable and looked anything but vicious. It looked useful. Practical. Lara stood in front of her dresser mirror and located the ridges along her neck where the talons within performed their surreal finger-painting. She dug the point of the boning knife in, flattened the blade, and described a clean slice down the length of a rubbery cord of sinew. She didn't see the blood ooze and then pulse from the manipulated orifice. She didn't feel the delicious sting. She only heard the wheezing melancholic sigh which escaped through the red sheets of her wound. A sirenic song which stopped the rolling tide and seduced her into its utopian shore with answers, so many answers all wrapped in that solitary sound. A single warm dirge, a hymn which ran out from the suppuration and wrapped itself, like a holy wimple, around her head, writhing through her ears and into her mind, teasing her nerve root and fucking her brain. Lara's head snapped backward, a tentatively connected cord of tendon snapping with it, spitting blood onto her eye as it shot upward. She stood, head back, eyes rolled up, mouth open, tongue lolling. A violent convulsion wracked her and she fell forward against her mirror. Though her pupils were turned far back into her head, facing her brain, she could see in the mirror the fingers regressing into the network of cables in her throat. And she could see herself. And she could see what she wanted to saturate in. She rattled out a pitiless sigh. This she could not see. This she did not need to.

She remembered when she first saw him. He was

dancing with his head lolling backwards on a fragile axis, a swan neck structured with thick tree root veins. A dichotomy of the sturdy and the fragile, the translucently ethereal and the grotesquely organic. She remembered his lolling head because she immediately thought it indicated the backward-thrust explication his face would express when he had sex.

She was always thinking ahead.

Lara wasn't a very good Catholic girl. She was the second to last virgin in her eleventh year at high school. The Catholic reputation for carnal voracity had seemingly escaped her. When her madonna was relinquished for the magdalene Lara was astounded at the intimate proximity between the human and the pig, specifically in their shared mastery of the grunt and its various incarnations. Perhaps this is why the sigh seemed so very beautiful and she became so very covetous. Back to the boy.

Lara leaned against a shadowy wall at the club watching this creature dance in ignorance of his screamingly attractive vulnerability. She smirked, half in disgust, half amused as she realised that, for the first time in her life, she was being nonchalant. She didn't even know what the literal translation of the word was, though she had learnt French for three years (too long). She leant her elbows over her uncomfortably exposed breasts, her hands pointed up, resting on her neck. The fingerings from the inside had recurred, and the only way to free the sighs within was to slice them an escape vent. It didn't hurt in a malignant way, but it looked terrible. She tried to hide the disarray of wound and scab that was her neck. Lara's confidence at being a vixen was less than outstanding. It made her ill at ease, like De Quincey's psycho-hallucinated theology. But remembering his writing, Lara felt a nerve of power tapped. She was fully aware it was all Victorian onanistic propaganda. Except the sigh. He had divined it and she was going to seek it out. Locate her inexplicable interest. Locate it in the undulating larynx that protruded from this boy's neck.

Lara was so far out of her depth procuring him (say it, *picking him up*) that all she could think about until they were alone naked in the dark together was what not to say to him. She mustn't say why she had chosen him, what she wanted through him, with him, in him. A musty smell of old clothes and the sighs of her sister as in childhood she slept, in the bed next to Lara, came to her. Infantile smells. Another smell. Flies. Lots and lots of flies. But what do flies smell like? This was her last thought as his warm, beautifully carved arms enveloped her.

Sex. Pain. The look was the step before the sigh. Not the transient sigh of lust, though that certainly appealed to her urge to gaze. She most certainly loved the ripe breaths he expelled into her ear, as he grew more vulnerable for her. But the thrill was only a prelude (kind of like faking it, thought Lara). The real, last sigh and its multiple relations, anguish, fear and trauma, were immeasurably more satisfying. Her fingertips moulded around his windpipe, stroking in rhythm with her flourishing visions. No, satisfaction is insubstantial. This was far, far down the path of experience. She was deeply in love with the noises this warm creature was making as they both fell away from where they were.

She didn't realise how far she had gone until she was too far gone to desist. She had felt those young sighs while he made love to her (made love, yeah right, while he fucked her). She was desperately trying to civilise the visceral motives behind the whole experience and failing abysmally. She had grown insatiably thirsty to hear them louder, more desperate, more varied in their inspiration. Lust was a little two-dimensional, she thought. Lust, confusion, disbelief, shock, fear, hopelessness. A glimpse of the wet, lightly coloured spectrum of the sigh.

Her fingers, which had only moments ago caressed him as gently as tendrils of web, pressed harder and harder for that noise. She was feeling like a desperate pubescent boy digitally penetrating his first girlfriend. They were viciously persistent, fingering the pulsating muscle and sinew, palpating for the exact spot that would release the sigh. Pushing, forcing, grimacing. Sigh, sigh, sigh, you fucker. Smiling, bruising, blood. When she felt viscous wetness flow over her hands she realised her fingers were submerged up to the second knuckle on either side of his trachea. Torn skin, tiny worms of vesicle and thick blood welled around her joints. He was no longer undulating in the rhythm of sex, he was convulsing. She hadn't realised where one ended and the next began except the end of creative sex heralded the beginning of desire. His deep, placid breaths had emerged from the cocoon of his throat deafening, gloriously transmuted. They licked her auricle and writhed into her auditory canal like parasites searching for warmth. Here was a body beneath her, pleading to her, for her. For her grace. For her mercy. But grace was found only in his rattling gifted breath. His trauma made him grow louder, yet who or what he was now seemed so far from the noises he engineered. She could hear his eyes glazing over. She had teased from his fibre the most perfect thing he could ever create. The carmine glossy buds of her exposed nerve endings received gruelling satiation. They shuddered like little anemone in a watery womb. They ejaculated an amphetamine which can only be inspired by the smell of real pleading confrontation. When he screams and tries to locate reason but reason isn't in the same genus as what makes the bitter flavour in fear-sweat taste so good. At his final emittence Lara heard her first and most beautiful death rattle. She lowered her head close to his arched throat, and lunging her mouth over his protruding thyroid muscle, tore the bulb from its socket, wanting to ingest the gelatinous origin of the sigh. She drank of it deeply and was still intoxicated with it long before she realised his grace had stilled.

Thou shalt not covet. Covet what? thought Lara. A sigh isn't really material. You can't *keep* it, though by hearing the strength of that indescribable one you could certainly be considered the owner of it. So did she covet? You can't keep sex, but you can certainly covet it day and night. But then, that has a whole 'Thou shalt not' of its own. And, (she was really teasing her rhetoric skills to their last thread here) the saving virtue which balances covetousness is generosity. She gave them a pinion of experience unlike anything they could ever have previously hoped to achieve. She was exquisitely giving.

Her need was not malevolent. Indeed it was amoral, without signification, only want. Nonetheless she especially liked the ones who claimed, under their 'dark' and supposedly anti-social veneer, to welcome all that was unusual and alternate. Because they always bit their lips the hardest trying to reclaim their pain, to make themselves sick gorging on their own misery, only to find the taste bilious and eventually throw it up a thousand-fold. Surely they should understand that they were not meant to cope with it, to withstand it. They were, ideally (though most were decidedly lacking idea, let alone ideology) meant to let it envelop them. It was the last physical, (and the religious cynic in Lara guessed spiritual) experience. It may as well be memorable. No, that sounded sickeningly apathetic (the apathetic, now they were fun). It should be viscerally and cerebrally unbearable, only they have no choice, they *have* to bear it.

De Quincey had insinuated that the greatest implement toward experience was the flesh. Of darkness, tears and sighs, surely the last belonged most implicitly to the human form. Darkness concealed corporeality. Tears came from the flesh, true, but they did not have so many incantations. They did not contort and discern between love and pain. Their hue remained stagnant. Lara was certainly impressed with tears, from the eyes, from the pores. But she didn't gorge on them. She never received from them the exultation that injected into her as the sighs of alarm caressed the cornucopia of her ear. She was their succubus, sucking them dry, but she stole no semen from these objects. Only their musical gasps, which existed indefinitely. Long after they had stopped writhing and turning, the gases which held their bodies rigid escaped, each creating a sound of corruption as unique as a fingerprint.

Lara made herself sick on sighs. She was too far obsessed with the procuring of the sounds and the heat to be concerned at the gravity of the carrion build-up in the crawl-space beneath her home. Those mothers are as other triumvirate female conflagrations, three muses, three graces, three fates and three furies. Mothers, not of children and without germinating males, mothers of human intensities incapable of creating, yet holding over life... Mater Suspiriorum, the mother of sighs and the oldest of the three... She herself... Just as there are...her others...

Lara was accidentally watching a junk Italian movie about the three mothers. Strange to think that these mythical figures are obviously pagan, probably Greek, but the film was named after a Catholic concept of hell. Some things it seems, transgress religious and chrono-logical boundaries. Next to Lara lay a youth with shiny black hair cut like a girl. A little part of her hoped he might still be alive. He had beautiful eyebrows and for-tunately had succumbed with his eyes open, so the visage was kept intact. She stroked his forehead lovingly, and pressed her thumb and forefinger firmly against his dia-phragm. He emitted a glorious expulsion of sound, as if the last demon of his imperfection was being exorcised.

She trailed her tongue over his lips, the last object the sigh had touched. She touched his drying eyeballs with her index finger, and pushed the pupil back into his head so only the whites were exposed. She liked that. It made her feel less guilty, less like they had a life before her. She glanced back to the television. Someone had just been severed in the throat by a pane of glass in which she could probably see her own reflection. Her punishment for hearing things she shouldn't have been listening to. The scraping in Lara's neck returned. The many bodies in the crawl-space rolled their eyes backward and groaned uncomfortably.

Something had been born inside Lara. At night, as she lay in bed clutching her asthma medication and scratching her throat, her mother came and told her. She never remembered crossing the morphean river from wakefulness to sleep, but rational thought told her that what was happening to her happened only in dreams. In dreams the fingers within her moved all over her body, inscribed her from the inside. Wrote on her in mirror writing, so that whatever was on the inside could read it, but she had to stand in front of her dresser to decipher the words. Not words, really. Sounds. Sounds that she could read etched across her welted and livid red torso. Articulations of covetousness from the lungs' tunnel. An Orphean tunnel perhaps.

She stood, naked and bare-souled, smothered in bloody, backward writing, ventolin clutched tightly in one hand, the other scratching her tortured neck, like an iconographised martyr loaded with potent symbols.

Her visage would be entirely at home up on a church ceiling. Rarely, however, did she have the serene look of the martyr on her face. Rather her look was of potential horror. Of fear at what was in her, how it was utilising the sighs it had gotten her addicted to, and what it ultimately wanted with her.

And her mother came to her in these dreams.

Not her birth mother, who had been all but useless as a role model in childhood. Mother Suspiriorum. The incantation of the suffering of man's heart, the meekness that belongs to hopelessness, clothed in human attributes, as presented with sighs. Of despair, of misery, of futility, beyond death, of nothingness.

For her, of pleasure.

This mother of sighs was her mother now. She had suckled Lara on nipples of warm air escaping from dying bodies. Lara's pleasure at this suffering transubstantiated into sustenance for something else. Something developing within her. Something whose body nestled within her thorax, between her ribs, and reached up to traumatise her vulnerable neck when it wanted more. It was as much an addict as her. And now it was writing on her, becoming articulate. Evolving.

Lara heard whispers in these myopic moments. Sighs not of primal substance but of explicit knowledge. Sighs that told her she would soon be living in walls, tempting people through plasterboard but never receiving sustenance. Sighs that explicated to her every implicit moment and pinnacle of despair ever felt by her victims (not my victims, I *gave* to them). These sighs would entwine around her and suffocate her, becoming her shroud. For her mother told her that the souls of the dead pass on, but the agony of their sighs remain.

If heaven is a place of pure happiness and the persecuted find only euphoria there, where does their suffering reside?

Lara was sweating heavily. She still heard them. They were dead but they were whispering. They writhed around beneath her in the crawl-space, occasionally thumping a head or appendage against their roof, her floor. Beneath her bed. She could still smell them. How many were there? Twelve? Around twelve... Not that many. And she had loved each one, taught each one. Lara's rhetoric was getting desperate. In the labyrinth of her mind the perfect world of sighs and flesh she had created was cannibalising itself. Engorging and vomiting, despising its own bitter taste. Only the dead flesh would be digested, and digested for eternity, forever being churned and smothered in the acidic gall of something that once tasted sweet...

They had all tasted sweet, especially the first. She had objectified them so well that the thought of their reanimated autonomy frightened her beyond her own comprehension. The creature in her body screamed and clawed to be let loose. Lara was being persecuted from within and without. Her abdomen spewed forth crimson bile from the frantic scrawling occurring within it. She cast her impossibly wide eyes down, their surface glazing as she read inscribed upon her own mutinous flesh

You are their Mother. Their suffering shall be your own.

The Mother she was wanted it. The creature inside her had wanted it. The youths had wanted it really. Pleasure had fallen into her hands and now it was burning her. The intestinal contortions which had accompanied indescribable pleasure were, as she lay there, eviscerating her. The skin of her belly grew tight and glossy, slick with blood. The boys beneath the floorboards bayed like insane cattle. The thing in her would not emerge but it could manipulate her from within. It threw her up out of her bed and against the wall. The plaster behind her splintered in a complicated vein pattern. Her head broke through the surface and she felt the ribs in her back individually crack as the thing pushed her brutally, from within, into the wall. Contusion smothered her. Blood ran from her hair into her eyes and clouded her vision as she passed out.

Lara woke from a dream. Into a dream. Her nose was pressed against a crumbly hard surface, the back of her head tightly forced against another. She couldn't move forward or backward. Though she was free on either side of her. If she pouted she could caress and lick her plaster sarcophagus with her mouth. When she blinked, her lashes scraped the suppressive prison's forewall. It hurt to move sideways because the rough wall grazed her cold, naked front. She couldn't see, it was pitch. Tiny bugs and silky cobwebs traced roadmaps over her. She hated their almost-there sensation. She felt so nauseous. The back of her throat tickled with bile and the urge to vomit. Lara could hear sighs, but they came from inside her head.

For she was suffering. God how she was suffering. She was experiencing the pain, anguish, torment, despair of a dozen people, but she couldn't run from it, block her ears, shut her eyes. It was explicitly located within her. Lara felt as if her eyes were rolled entirely back into her head and watching a horror movie – without images, only intensities – on a screen in her brain. Where the sounds and emotions were all real. Etched forever into her soul.

Then the fingers came. Not from inside, but worse, from the tiny space where Lara's feet rested on the earthy floorboards. Rubbery, coagulated fingers of long dead boys with so much agony to give, so much life to take from her. Where their souls were she couldn't know, but here was their oblivion, desolate sighs which she had birthed, parthenogenesis of despair. The tininess of the space made their touch unbearable, it was so much more acute and poignant than if she had been entirely marauded by them. Their fingertips traced and teased the underside of her disgusted skin. They licked her ankles with their hands, worrying her toes by wriggling their fingernails beneath her toenails. Her toes curled, her feet arched but there was no contortion she could perform to even lessen the intimacy of those cold umbilical fingers. Her biliousness grew extreme. In the tiny space between the walls Lara felt her hot, sighing breath bouncing back from the plaster into her face, making her tears turn cold. She could hear every single breath she took, each one like nails down glass, raspy, asthmatic. Rattling.

And then Lara opened her nostrils and drank in a familiar smell. Of mammal. Of warm, bloodied bodied house mice. In the wall with her. She grimaced as the smell rolled over the back of her tongue down her throat. She was choking on want. On longing. On something she could never have again and an eternity of anguish she did not want to receive. She coughed up phlegm that looked like fresh turned soil, which crumbled over her lips down her front. She widened her cracking mouth and tried to scream.

The sound came out as silent affliction.

'She weeps not. She groans not. But she sighs inaudibly at intervals'.

The sound came out as a sigh.

From him deep in the nerve is given
the love and the blood drunk, that before
the old wound dries, it bleeds again.
My eye must not be polluted by the last
gaspings for breath.

– Aeschylus *Agamemnon*

She

Brian G. Ross

I see her everywhere. In the park. In the supermarket. Drinking coffee in Starbucks.

She wears sweats and an iPod: she wears a skirt and high heels. Her hair is brown, maybe blonde; sometimes straight, sometimes not. I watch her ride the bus. I watch her drive a car. When she walks, it is with a different dog every day.

She is on cereal boxes and billboards. She is lost on milk cartons. Every television commercial, she sings the jingles. I see her form in the clouds, and when the stars come out I join the dots and she is there. Her reflection is in the water, her shape is in my shadow.

When I read a book, she is between the lines. I look in the mirror and she stares back at me from behind the glass. I see her at the office; by the water cooler, in the canteen. Sitting at the desk next to mine.

I hear her voice in my sleep, turning my dreams sour. From across the street I can smell her perfume, but the wind has chased it away by the time I go to meet it. Sometimes I feel her poisoned whispers on the back of my neck; nothings that are not so sweet.

I see her underneath me while I fuck someone else.

Fuck her.

Someone else.

So I plucked out her eyes and sliced off her ears, cut off her tongue for begging me to stop, her hands for pushing me away, and her feet for trying to run. Enough was too much.

I keep the leftovers in a burlap sack.

But still, she will not let me be.

The Wait

Scott Stainton Miller

For a long time, sundered limbs have boomeranged through the blue sky, twirling, poorly thrown, too much gusto, not returning, going and going, spinning end over stump bearing flames to land in the dust for collection by worm conscious early birds, be they thieves or animals or clean-up crews with buckets and bags.

Then they're gone.

They are captured in flight, though, by cameras and we all watched these odd birds fly and it was pretty beautiful in a way. Some real dark joy there. But even at the start it was almost not shocking and then as the years began to seem less like colourful passages in which a great variety of things happened than thin tally marks on a wall so vast it was hard to see the whole, it went from almost not shocking to not shocking to oh...look...more of *that*.

And there they still were, born of flames, dust-bound.

I turned off the television and went to bed.

The upstairs neighbour's child was screaming again. She was six and such a screamer. It was a sound that I would never become used to. It was an inhuman sound. Not at all normal. It was guttural, deep and sustained and it had many peaks and valleys. I began to think she was being raped by her parents.

They had taken their carpets up four months previous and I now heard them farting, coughing, pissing, shitting, shifting weight from foot to foot, speaking, snoring, *everything*. There was an inch or two of poorly insulated space between us. They were living on my ceiling now. Everything they did I was witness to with my ears. I'd spoken to them, written them letters, and been rebuffed each time as some kind of cunt.

It was something I was trying to learn to live with until I could afford to move out. But I *kept* hearing their child screaming and it truly sounded to me like she was being raped. I would hear them creaking around in her room at night; quick, agitated footsteps, a muffled groan or two, a shuffle, a thump.

So much screaming.

At first it seemed like she was merely a difficult child, reared as a keening piglet by two mash-faced uteral scrapings, and that was it and that was all. There were shouts and protestations at bed times and bath times. I would hear the child pleading and whining to skip baths, to stay up late and have more ice cream.

But then the words left and all that remained was screaming, until one night I heard them above me in their living room. It sounded as though it was raining bones up there. A storm of knuckles, a blizzard of ribs. I heard the woman's voice, then the man's. They were angry, urgent

and merciless. I heard the child pleading over and over
No Daddy No – No Daddy No – No Daddy No.

Then the words left and did so forever. Just screams
now. Every day.

I didn't know what to do.

I could have been overreacting, over-thinking. If I called
the police, what then? Recrimination, hatred, *retaliation*. If
I called the police; besmirching, name-smearing, shit-sticking.
Parents cast as sinister, demoniac, libidinous and sick.

I turned up the volume on the news and the limbs
flew before the eruption sounded out and I waited for
the bang rendered as a pop by the flat sounding television and I watched and watched and waited for the
screaming up above and the thumping all around to
please just *stop* and it did after a while and by that time
it was dark and I was tired so I turned off the television
and went to bed.

I had no real reason to call the police. I said this a
lot in my head and then out loud, enough to make it
feel like a *real* decision with *real* weight behind it; an
adult's decision. The right one.

One night was particularly bad. I had to leave the flat
and walk around for a while in the dark, scared of shadows
and youths with knives and sulphate scabs around their
cracked and burning mouths. I'd seen them, roaming
around, bellowing at each other, at passers-by, and I kept
my head down always, but in the dark and past the witching
hour, I was bleakly aware that the tilt of my neck was perfect for cutting, that the weight of my head would snap the
sinews and then just drop to the concrete to break and

leak with ripped vocal cords jabbering through the foam.

I was unmolested. I thanked a God I never thought about and went to bed.

The next morning I woke to a weird looking day. Silvery, draped. I got up, washed, the usual, but I was hungry. I wanted meat. There was nothing in the fridge but eggs and an old hamburger that had moved through its initial stage of malodorous mulch into something better, more unusual. It was now dwelling in its own strange, shell-like chrysalis.

Sighing, I reached in and pulled a couple of eggs from the carton, cracked them on the side of a bowl and emptied them out, a strong feeling of déjà vu squirming in my bowels.

The bowl was filled with blood: thick, yolk-streaked blood. I tipped it into the sink and cracked another egg. More blood, this time with a small brown twist of nascent chick. Gagging, I threw the gelatinous mess into the bin and fetched the rest of the eggs from the fridge. I broke them into the carton and watched, appalled, as the rough cardboard pockets filled with oily dark red liquid.

The imagery remained with me on the train, the expression on my face causing the other commuters to form a berth around me.

When I stepped from the train it was like I was being pulled, clasped, and wrenched forth. I was fast, slippery, moving piscine and free through the first reeking crowd of our great working day. I looked at the station's clock. I was early for work. A first.

My insides felt cold.

I bought a coffee and sat on a stone bench, encased in a beam of hot morning light. I was halfway through the coffee when a tramp sat next to me and started to talk. I tensed, unsure how to get up and leave without offending the man.

'Beautiful morning,' he said. His face looked like an old letter, crushed, stained brown with age and veined over with deep, unusual wrinkles as though he'd been tallying the days by cutting clean, deep ravines into his forehead and face.

'Sure is,' I said, wary of creating conversation.

'It's a nice time of year. The weather has *never* been better.'

'Yup.'

'I'm going to sit here *all day* and *enjoy* it.'

'Right... I have to go to work.'

'That's a shame. Beautiful day like this... You know, everywhere people are dying. *Everywhere*.'

'Yes. I do know. Well...*bye*.'

'May I ask you something?'

I stood and rooted through my pockets for change.

'Do you think that's how it's supposed to be?' said the tramp.

I stopped rooting and frowned. 'I don't know. Look,' I said 'I don't really have any change...'

'I don't want your money,' said the man, eyes dropping to the ground.

'Sorry. I just...'

'It was nice talking to you,' said the tramp, eyes still lowered.

I mumbled an apology and turned away.

Feeling guilty, I arrived at my office, and ground the day away, pausing only to complain about my neighbours and to entreat opinion from people I could never consider as peers about the rightness of my *not* alerting the authorities. They agreed and that was all I wanted so I went home happy.

The kid screamed for a while and then everything went silent at eight thirty. This became the norm. Screaming and then silent by eight thirty. I started to go to the pub after work with my co-workers. I would leave them at eight and be home in time for no-more-screaming, for silence. Relative silence, I mean. I still could hear them moving around.

Everything was better.

Until I heard her crying *No Not Anymore, I Can't, Daddy, I Can't.*

My stomach dropped.

I heard him grunting and swearing and telling her to shut up, to just shut up and take it.

'Medicine,' I said out loud. 'She doesn't want to take her *medicine*. She is ill and her medicine tastes bad and... that's *it*.'

My words sounded fake, like a bad line reading, and I did my best to pretend I believed it and I realised that above everything, above my doubts that nothing bad was happening, above the desperate trembling belief that I was paranoid, above all *that*, I just could not bear to get involved. And that was it.

That was all.

The next morning was a beautiful morning. I had

risen earlier than usual, and I did not feel refreshed, so I decided to walk through the nicer parts of town in order to feel free and unrushed and alone. It was five o' clock. I began work at eight. In all of town, there was only me and a hot new sun so bright it was silver. I could see it through the haze of its own heat, burning so clean and new and circular it was like a neat hole punched through to a paradise beyond.

I bought coffee from a shop that wasn't open yet (the owner took pity on me, he said, due to the perfect dark circles under my burning red eyes), and then strolled along very slowly, sipping at the strong, black liquid and enjoying the lack of ideas in my mind.

I stopped.

The tramp I'd offended weeks ago was sitting on a marble bench, his back to me. He was singing to himself. This was a chance, I thought, a chance to apologise, to *redeem*. He stopped singing as my shadow spread over him, and he turned.

His eyes were bleeding.

I could not speak.

'Morning, son. And it *is* a beautiful morning, is it not? 'Course, I'm looking at everything through rose tinted spectacles. Of a kind... You know, you're terribly familiar. Have we met?'

I was finding it hard to breathe correctly. He looked at me, smiling, eyes coursing.

'Are you *alright*?' I managed. 'Do you want me to call you an ambulance?'

'No I'm *not* alright,' he said. 'I'm not alright *at all*.'

I barely heard him, I was too distracted by the blood. It was seeping steadily over his puffy lower lids and moving in neat stripes down his cheeks.

I took a step back, grimacing as the sheer ridiculousness of asking a man whose eyes are pouring with blood if he requires medical help suddenly struck me. 'Yes, I'll, *sorry*, I'll... I'll get an *ambulance*,' I said.

'I've seen a lot,' he said. 'Saw someone murdered. Even a rape. That one...that one was worse, somehow. Worse than the murder. When it happened, I...' he stopped and shook his head, unable to part with the terrible fullness of his past.

My bowels felt heavy, leaden, full to bursting.

The tramp grabbed my wrist, making me drop the coffee, and shook his head, blood washing wider down his face with each shake.

'I do not require an ambulance,' he said. 'I take care of myself. I can take care of myself.'

I had nothing to say. There was nothing to say. Or think. The moment was holding me prisoner.

'I'll just take care of it,' said the man, letting go of my wrist.

'But...'

'Relax, son. It's a beautiful day,' he said. Then he took his forefingers, and, with two short stabbing motions, hooked the tips under and behind his eyes. The noise was small and discreet, two slurps. Grunting, the tramp pushed them in, hooking, curling, his knuckles knocking loud against the hard bone-back of the sockets, and then he just...pulled them out.

They came with a wet, flatulent noise and dangled half burst against his cheeks.

'See,' said the tramp.

'I...' I said and that was all. Words were elusive. Words often are. And whatever is said in moments of extreme stress usually sound fake. *What the _fuck_. Jesus _Christ_. Oh my _God_.* Everything overemphasised. 'What the fuck.' I said. 'Jesus Christ.' I said. 'Oh my God.' I said, then: 'I'll get an ambulance. I'm... I'm sorry. I'll get an ambulance.'

The tramp raised his hands to his cheeks and pulled at the trailing optic nerves as though he were pushing lank locks of hair aside. He yanked and they came away in his hands. He threw them on the pavement where they broke like rotten eggs.

'It's a beautiful day,' he said, voice thick as though drunk. His eyelids, so horribly redundant, quivered like the frilled edges of a snail. His face went slack as though its strings had been cut and he hit the ground as a wet sack of spoilage.

I did the same.

When I awoke, a woman was leaning over me, peering. She had a curious kind of expression. Irritation, I think.

I realised I was lying down and sat up, almost butting heads with the woman.

'Do you need an ambulance?' she asked.

I shook my head and pointed to the spot where the tramp had collapsed, now empty. The blood still remained though, and the eyes, although they had been smooshed into the concrete as though stamped on and *dragged*.

Really, the viscera was indistinguishable from the slime that collects in the corners of derelict doorways and in each and every alley of an evening.

'Did you faint? Did you throw up and faint?' asked the woman. She sounded bored.

'That's *blood*,' I said.

'Is it yours?'

'No.'

'Well, it's *not* mine, so...'

The woman nodded and shrugged her shoulders. She didn't say goodbye. I stood and stared at the goo. It began to rain. The church in the square began to sound out the time. It was nine o'clock. I had no way to process what I'd just seen and nobody to answer to, so I went to work and sat behind my desk and waited for someone in a position of authority, someone whose job it was to ask questions, to call me, to ask me, and the day passed like normal and nobody called, so I went home and I lay down on my couch and waited for 8:30.

The screaming wouldn't stop and I waited for the phone to ring for the screaming to stop for sleep to come for questions to be asked and things to be done but I was waiting for nothing and oh God the screaming would not stop. I heard her crying out for help. And then I heard nothing and that was so beautiful I cried I was so grateful.

I was so grateful.

I did not sleep though. The marbles in my head were lithopedians, rolling around like a million billiards, one for every scream, and they cracked hard against the insides of my skull, keeping me awake.

When the sun came up I pulled myself out of bed and I wrote a letter, which I did not sign.

All it said was this: What are you doing to her?

I stepped out of my flat in nothing but my boxer shorts and I walked up the cold stone steps and stood outside their door with the letter in my hand. There was a red smudge on their white doorframe.

I put the letter through the letterbox and returned to my flat to get dressed and go to work like normal.

On the train, broadsheet newspapers hung wide open like eldritch butterflies stunned in the foglike funk of our great morning stench and they didn't tell me anything about dead tramps or eye sockets or rape or bombs or anything so I went to work like normal and I sat there ignoring everybody because they made me sick and I kept thinking they all looked alike, like milk-fed andro-gynes with no teeth or bones or hair or moles or birth-marks scars or angles and that's when I started sweating blood. Just a little. It stained the armpits of my shirt red. So I put my jacket on and told everyone that yes, I was cold. They told me I was probably coming down with something and I agreed with them. My boss said I should take some time off and I told him no I wouldn't know what to do with myself all day ha ha.

He sent me home anyway. I didn't thank him.

I stood in the shower watching the red water swirling into the plug. I turned the cold water up till I was numb and the water seemed a lot less red so I dried off and sat in the lounge. It was a while before I realised I couldn't hear anything. Not a single thing.

No footsteps, no creaking like the belly of an ageing pirate's ship, no nothing.

Nothing.

I sat there and waited and waited for nothing.

I sat there all night. Then all day and all night and on and on and I pissed and shat where I sat and I waited and did not eat or move and there was only nothing.

Nobody came to my door and my phone did not ring and no letters were delivered. My hearing became so acute I could hear the silverfish under the floorboards moving, their antennas slicing through the air and batting away the floating particles of dust they disturbed as they strolled through the hidden filth beneath my feet.

But nothing else.

I stood up. My clothes were brown with perspired blood. I washed. I went back to work. I wore a black shirt and trousers. I sat with a fan whirring and the window open. I barely moved. There was a light red sheen on my forehead. But that was all and nobody saw.

When I got home I noticed that my bedroom ceiling was sagging. It was hardly noticeable, just a slight swell, but I saw it anyway. I peeled off my clothes and stood in front of the mirror. My body was sticky with blood, shining. I smiled and broke into a series of star-shapes, arms up arms down arms up arms down legs open shut open shut open shut. Blood began to pour out from under my hair, to drip from my armpits and forearms, from my balls and arse. It was pissing from me, running down me, painting me, staining the carpet. It ran into my eyes, into my teeth. No part of my body wasn't slick with it, wasn't heavy with congealing skeins of it.

I lay down on the floor underneath the sagging ceiling and felt the blood caking on me, scabbing. I closed my eyes and slept while up above me the sag grew in size, and grew and grew and still I lay beneath it, dreaming that I was watching it swell and darken and split and a river of rotten blood and skin and bone and ruptured eyes sluiced through it, slopping onto me, dead and writhing and alive and full of sundered limb murder rape and broken child and it wound around me like a cocoon and mixed its blood with mine and I have not woken since but I am quite aware and I am many now and more awake than ever and I move so fast like a flood and yes, I am coming for you.

Lost

Sam Thewlis

The night is crisp and clear, smoky breath pluming in the chill. Something is banging in a breeze, a door or window enlivened by rogue gusts of wind.

It is dark outside, one light on in one room. Peculiar shadows are cast on the wall, as the standard lamp is lounging in a particularly laid-back fashion, a far cry from its normal military posture.

The room is dishevelled, the contents of the coffee table in swathes across the floor, bits of broken plant pots and soil trodden into the carpet. No bookcase has its full complement of residents, only one still at a usable angle, the casualties littering the floor, broken spines and torn covers galore. A stain on the anaglypta, orange and red, could be beans, could be ketchup, could be something else. Something has spilled on the carpet, something sticky, that has attracted bits of fluff and dust, and incongruously, a long forgotten dice.

She is sitting in an awkward heap, legs splayed in an uncomfortable fashion. There is a gaping ladder in one leg of her tights, revealing tender flesh, raw and naked, scraped and sore. She is huddled, not in a ball, more like a pile of arms, wild hair, cardigan and shoes. Her sobs have the weary quality of those that were once fraught and urgent, but that have now faded to a despondent musak. Her face is grimy, tracks of her tears evidence of her obvious pain. Her hair is matted, tangled and there is blood, likely hers, tinting the roots. Her eyes are squeezed tightly shut, pinched with the vaguest hue of blue giving the impression she has bruised them with tears.

It is very still now, almost eerily so, the gathering darkness pervading each room in turn. As she sits, hunched on the floor, she has a sudden, stomach turning recollection of sunnier times spent in this room. She can almost feel the warm sun of their first summer in this house, see the golden glow coating everything in syrupy sepia, although this is probably wistfulness rather than actual recall. In her mind's eye she can see him as he hugged her and spun her round in his arms when he came home with news of his promotion, making her feel tiny and girlish and fun. She remembers the champagne, bubbles tickling her nose when he closed that big deal, remembers him pouring the icy drink down her smooth calves as she lay upside down on the floor, legs on the sofa, inviting.

She can see his face the day she told him the good news, the momentous news, that they were going to become parents, strictly speaking already were. The shock and bewilderment swiftly clearing to expose the pure, unadulterated joy she had not truly been expecting.

She knew as soon as she saw her son that he was the most amazing thing she had ever produced. She also knew that, when she passed him his son, she had forsaken her place in his heart forever. She just knew. The same way she immediately understood she was not a natural mother, that the love of a small child would not compensate her for the loss of a man.

And that was where it all started to unravel. Little by little, piece by piece her life disintegrated, leaving her slumped lifelessly near the wreckage of the coffee table.

He is gone now. She felt his absence keenly, the news of his departure like a proverbial punch to the gut. He never used his physicality against her, though she had sometimes wished he would, either to shatter his perfect memory, or to confirm her imperfections. Sometimes she wondered whether things might have been different if he had roughed her up a bit.

Her solicitor told her he wants custody. She imagined a thick, gloopy yellow liquid slopping over his head. She dared not laugh though for fear she be thought crazy, or worse, prove it so. So she has fought, as directed, yet without the fight required.

Her nails are ragged and torn, but whether from trauma or daily gnawing is impossible to tell. Her cardigan is ripped and hanging limply from a bony shoulder. Her chest heaves with her sobs, and with a deeper sense of sorrow of something lost forever.

And there he is, lying peacefully at her feet, urgently quiet, eyes closed but lacking the violent pressure needed to keep them shut. He looks angelic, as all small children do when asleep, until they awaken and begin attacking the world as they do every morning. As most children do every morning.

His hair is a little rumpled, almost as if he has just got up, with a small cowlick just flopping over his forehead at one corner, as if to emphasise his total cuteness.

His skin shows the telltale marks of bruising, faint blue and purple shadows already gathering strength. With one hand she is caressing his hair, letting the silky fronds slip through her fingers in a continuous soothing motion. Her other hand is in her lap, worrying a hangnail, her cardigan, the hem of her skirt. This hand is frantic, ceaseless and remorseless, picking at skin to make it bleed, picking an already unravelled hem.

She looks at him through her watery lashes, and there is genuine deep love there. A low moaning emanates from somewhere far inside her, a sore keening like an animal in pain, a mother mourning her child. Her shaking fingers caress his cheek, drawing a trail of tears. He is still so warm, his cheeks still bearing a rosy bloom.

Tears roll down her nose, landing heavily on his face, pooling by his mouth. She has nothing left now, no possessions, no more to give, no reason for going on. She looks at her child, still marvelling at the pure wondrousness of him. She had never quite come to terms with the enormity of what she had been given, and now it was too late.

She continues to sob, silently, her body racked with guilt, shaking and rocking. The room is quiet, save for the irregular tick tick tong of the erstwhile mantel clock, now languishing in several pieces on the floor.

She had had such high hopes for him, a glittering career in film or television, or a sportsman, dashing and debonair, a credit to his modest, yet marvellous mother, the constant support in his life. Except it hadn't quite worked out like that. Her mothering skills, far from coming naturally, had stuttered and stumbled. Torn between the guilt of wanting to spend all her time with him and the knowledge that she couldn't bear to, she slipped into a dark place, darker than the blackest of nightmares, darker than the point of a full stop. And just when she had thought she had no emotion left, no toss left to give, she discovered, when faced with the absolute worst, that something was left, a mere spark in the pitch, but enough. Enough to realise how truly lost she was.

Then, a small shuddering intake of breath, followed by a weak, but audible wail. She stops, holds her breath, gazing in disbelief at her tiny son. He wriggles a little, not opening his eyes, but writhes on the floor, in distress or discomfort is unclear, but he is incredibly, indisputably alive.

She lets her breath go with a quiet cough, tears drying on her face. She leans over the baby, and strokes his chest with the tenderest of touches, before gathering up the fabric in her lap. It was once the belt from her cardigan, now somewhat torn and tatty. One last tear escapes her determined gaze as she slips the belt around his throat, into the matching imprints already blushing with colour, the earlier bruising evident. And gently, but firmly, she tightens her grip.

Keeping Someone

Samuel Minier

Gone.

Right, sure. What ridiculous – whose fucking idea is that? Just because you're not here, then we're through?

Not what we tell the grieving. 'Just close your eyes and still, your loved ones are with you.' Right? So what difference is there, between hiding a body in a box and keeping you in my head?

Not like I had a choice. Forever with me when we were together, and now – Jesus Christ. Now there's nothing but the wind playing with your hair when we first met. Your crimson scent on New Year's. The gentle drop of your collarbone under my lips. All these pieces of you, patch-worked into some golem shambling eternally behind me.

Get over it? Move on? I could drive to the fucking moon and still your monster would come, each step click-tapping across that tile patio of that café in Newport. Pills can't cloud away your faces. All the other women wear your taste.

I refuse to be stalked by a dismembered you. Actually

a dis-REmembered you.

That's why I grabbed you that night, in the alley outside the club. A brief spin-tussle, your fear so ripe and
unnecessary. All I needed to say were three words. Not
so little, and not what you think – the first seven syllables,
the second longer, the last so contorted I ripped something in my throat pronouncing it. My mouth coppery,
your sleeve suddenly empty in my hand. The rest of your
clothes in a pile at my feet, and you – gone. Gone but
not forgotten.

I didn't want some chopped-up ghost. Needed you
whole – kept complete, completely in my head. Like
this.

Your fist-falls against the inside of my skull like cher-
ished migraines. Your screams like a little girl lost down
a dark hole.

Windchimes

Paul Kane

Sunday morning and the city is still asleep.

As he walks down the litter-strewn street, beer cans and bottles from the night before adorning its gutters, he encounters very few people. There is a noticeable lack of traffic on the main road, only one or two cars passing him by as he reaches those familiar wrought iron gates, the black paint peeling with age.

The pathway which runs down the centre of the park stretches out like a duller version of the Yellow Brick Road, and with considerably less promise. The grass on either side is neatly trimmed and a young couple arm-in-arm, wearing matching coats and scarves, are throwing a ball for their Labrador to the left of him. Ignoring the laughter, he hunches down in his dark greatcoat and cuts across the sea of green.

He hasn't been walking long when he comes across the place he's looking for, right where it always is. The stone markers are planted in rows, with just enough of a gap between each to allow people to walk down them. Some are large, some small; some are plain crosses or squares, others boasting carved angels playing trumpets. Many are weathered, time and the seasons doing their worst. On the oldest, the names are only just recognisable. On the new, all too legible.

When the rest of the city finally wakes, breaking into the routine of another lazy weekend day, these people will not. They will never wake again.

There are trees scattered here and there, as if to show that even in this place of death and mourning, there is new life. Yet, on this mid-autumn day, the leaves have begun their descent from their branches, to gather at the trunks, to be swirled around by the light breeze.

He carries on through the graveyard, barely glancing at these. He's heading for another section, one which is separated from the rest by another pathway. There is more colour here, to break up the greys and blacks. Splashes of reds, pinks and whites, where flowers have been left. But the plots are so much smaller than the ones across the way, no massive headstones; just tiny plaques.

The little rectangular graves are covered with cream and brown pebbles. A few have miniature fences around them, others latticed stone or marble marking off individual plots. But more than anything it is the toys that give the game away. Stuffed teddy bears, model cars and trucks, a doll's house lovingly painted (though now more than a little the worse for wear). Then the inscriptions: 'You'll always live on in our memories. Love forever, Mummy and Daddy.'; 'For a special little girl.'; 'You're only a thought away.' The dates show the oldest only to be about three or four.

Jon Cassidy knows them all too well, but doesn't read them anymore. He can't. Not because he's unfeeling, but because he can only hold so much sorrow in his heart. And that has been reserved for one very special plot.

In the relative shade of an oak tree he pauses, stands with his head bowed. Jon takes the small bunch of orange and yellow flowers he has been clutching and places them on the grave, next to a rattle. If there was anyone around to witness this, they would no doubt comment on his pallid skin, his sunken eyes – dry, because there were no more tears left to shed – the way his lip is trembling. Especially as he reads the writing on the plaque there: 'Emma Louise Cassidy. One year was all the time we had.'

More leaves fall from the tree above him, raining down, but he doesn't take any notice. It is only when a sound comes from above that he looks up. There, hanging from one of the branches, is a collection of windchimes. There are baubles, stars, one even in the shape of a tear – made from glass and silver that catches the early sunlight. But one stands out from the rest, lengths of metal dangling from a brass-coloured angel, more cherubic-looking than any of those in the main graveyard, which looks sadly down on him. It makes a distinctive sound, a tinkling seemingly louder than any of the others.

And when he sees this, Jon realises there are still tears left. There always will be. Eyes wet, and brushing away the consequences with the back of his hand, he whispers, 'I'm sorry.'

Head bowed again, he begins the long trek back

though the graveyard. Gravity feels denser, his body aches. When he reaches the park he finds that families are now gathering. Children play with Frisbees, mothers and fathers cheer them on. It should hurt to see them, but he simply shivers. He feels cold.

In his own way, Jon is just as dead as the corpses buried behind him.

That night Jon sits alone in his flat.

The living room is a shrine to the god Detritus. Around the armchair where he is slumped lies the evidence of how he has been living his life: the crisp packets, the cans of beer, the empty pizza boxes smeared with grease, bugs crawling in and out and feasting on the leftover food inside.

A snapshot, a moment in time; taken at another time, in another place, it would have been so different. Like the one in the frame on the table next to him, beside the half empty bottle of malt. Jon and a woman with blonde hair, his arm around her as she holds a bundle of blankets. And just visible, poking out of the top, a round, pink face, features screwed up, eyes barely open. Jon, his shirt untucked and a glass of brown liquid in his hand, picks up the frame and traces the woman's face with his finger, then the baby's.

Jon puts down the photo and picks up his cordless phone. Though he has the number on speed-dial, he presses the buttons anyway with his thumb. Jon remembers the number. After all, it used to be his own.

It rings several times before the phone at the other end is picked up. 'Hello,' echoes a woman's voice, slightly muffled.

'Claire... Claire, it's me.'

There's a painful silence and then: 'You've got to stop doing this, Jon.'

'I –'

'What do you want?' The edge to her voice sends shivers down his spine. He can remember a time when it did exactly the same, but they were pleasurable tingles, more often than not accompanied by colourful winged insects flapping around in his stomach. Today there's just a heavy weight in there.

'To talk.'

Claire sighs. 'We've done all our talking. Now I just want you to leave me alone.' Yes, leave her alone so that she could pretend none of this had ever happened, that they'd never even met, let alone...

'Please...listen...' Jon's words are a little slurred.

'Have you been drinking?'

Jon stares down at the glass. 'A bit.'

'For Christ's sake. I'm going now.'

'Please don't.'

He hears the sound of a scuffle down the phone line, then another voice, a man's voice. *Him*. Jon's replacement in her warped parallel universe. 'Give me that... You heard what she said. Claire's moved on. She's trying to make a new life for herself...I suggest you do the same.'

There's a loud click as the phone is slammed down

on its cradle. An indifferent *burrrrr* wafts over the line: it's dead. Jon lets the phone drop from his grasp, then drains the rest of the whisky from his glass. He looks down at the photograph, picks it up, and throws it across the room. There's a tinkling sound as it hits the wall. Jon begins to cry again, uncontrollably this time.

When he finally goes over to retrieve the photo – after waking in the middle of the night, soaking in sweat from his alcohol-induced coma – Jon sees a huge spider's web crack across the glass. It stems from Claire and Emma.

The days blend into each other, but he is back at the grave again soon. This time, crouching by a grave just up from the tree – second row along, at the end – Jon notices another figure out of the corner of his eye. He looks more closely: it's a woman dressed in a black coat, grey skirt, visiting one of the graves. Jon watches as she mirrors his own actions, laying flowers on the grave. They are the only two people around in the children's grave-yard, the only two who can take such a depressing place this early. Or maybe the only two who have nowhere else to go.

In the end, it doesn't really matter to Jon. He returns his gaze to Emma's grave. When he happens to look up again, the woman is gone.

There's a slight breeze and above him the windchimes jangle, the angel still looking down pitifully on him.

The distinctive tinkling sound reaches his ears.

✳

That night Jon arrives back at his flat, ignoring his angry landlady who wants to talk to him about the rent increase. He brandishes his bottle in the brown paper bag like a weapon, St George seeing off the fiery dragon. His landlady warns him that she won't put up with that kind of behaviour forever; one of these days he'll come back and find that the locks have been changed. Jon climbs the stairs and says nothing. It doesn't bother him if he's sleeping in a shop doorway by this time next week.

Jon enters his flat, kicking aside the carpet that has ridged up. When he passes the answerphone in the hall he sees that the red light is flashing. *Maybe it's her...*he thinks, clutching at straws. *Maybe she's changed her mind. Maybe we can start over, work through the problems?* He's willing if she is.

Eagerly, Jon presses the button and it beeps. When he hears the deep, throaty voice, his heart sinks again. 'Jon, it's Michael. Look, I know you've been going through a lot and I sympathise, I really do. It's just that we're really going to need those completed proofs soon. Otherwise it could mean – '

Jon presses the button again, turning off the drone. Next he deletes the message. *If only you could do that in the real world – delete then record over the top*, he thinks. Wipe out whatever has made you sad, broken you, left you clinging to the drain for fear of spiralling down it.

It's a nice fantasy, but reality isn't like that – and Jon

knows what he has to do to blot that out. He wanders into the kitchen, passing dirty pots piled high in the sink, a half-finished loaf of bread – now rock hard – and a tub of butter with the lid off, and grabs a mug from one of the cupboards overhead. He takes his bottle out of the brown paper bag, pours a generous amount into the mug, and takes a swig.

Jon's shoulders slump. He wonders whether he'll wake at all tomorrow, and thinks it's probably best if he doesn't.

And yet here he is again, back at the graveyard.

It's like he's become stuck in a loop, the plot of some silly science fiction anthology show. The same thing over and over again until it drives him insane. He isn't far away from that now anyway.

At the graveside, Jon is lost in his thoughts. The wind-chime – Emma's windchime – jangles softly above. Jon starts when he hears the voice, but only because he didn't hear the woman approach, didn't even realise she was in the graveyard.

'Oh, I'm sorry,' she says when he jumps. 'I didn't mean to...'

Jon composes himself, tells her it's okay, that he was miles away. He recognises her as the person he's seen here before, but never up close, never *this* close. She has copper hair which falls in ringlets and grey eyes: a strange combination but one that works remarkably well.

He wouldn't describe her as a natural beauty but she certainly has something. Jon can't help but stare. She catches his eye and he looks away.

'It's very beautiful,' the woman says.

'I'm sorry.' Jon follows her finger, to the windchime above Emma's grave.

'I...I was thinking of maybe getting one myself.'

Jon nods, unsure of how to respond to this. They lapse into silence. For the longest time nothing is said. The woman's eyes drop to the floor again and she turns as if to walk away and leave him to his thoughts. Suddenly, Jon realises he doesn't want that.

'There's...there's a reason people leave them there,' he blurts out.

She stops and turns back towards him. 'To remember.'

And that's true, she almost gets it, Jon can see that. But the children here will be remembered with or without them. 'It's more than that,' Jon tells her. 'They say that when someone...' He pauses, realising what he's going to say will sound really stupid. 'No, forget it.'

'Go on...please,' she encourages him, facing him fully now, the wind blowing a strand of that springy copper hair across her face. 'I want to know.'

'It's just that some people say that when someone dies, their spirits drift on the wind.'

She comes closer again, even nearer than before – towards the grave.

'And...' Jon continues, 'And some say when the wind-chimes jangle like that it's as if they're talking to us.'

She joins him, then looks up again at the branches. 'Do you think that's true?'

'I don't know. But I like to think so.'

She considers this for a moment, cocking her head, listening to the windchimes – listening to one in particular. 'I wonder what they're trying to tell us.'

Jon shrugs.

'You're here quite often, aren't you?' she says to him.

'I come as often as I can.'

Her eyes fall again, but this time she reads the plaque in front of her, mouthing the inscription. Jon feels a stab of pain in his heart and bites back the tears. He can't lose it now, not here, not in front of this stranger. Better to wait till he gets home again, better to wait till he has a drink in his hand. He grits his teeth, gaining some kind of control over himself.

To deflect attention away from himself, Jon asks, 'The grave down there...is it –'

He sees her stiffen, eyes narrowing.

'I'm sorry. I shouldn't have asked...'

Then, almost a whisper, she says, 'My son, Joshua.'

'I'm really sorry.'

She looks at him and he sees that she wasn't being defensive at all; she was trying to fight back the grief just like him. 'So am I... And your daughter... A year. No age at all.'

Jon shakes his head. 'No. How old was –'

'Four months.' Now a tear does escape and trickles down her cheek.

'Jesus,' says Jon, not feeling any guilt because of where he is. He finished with religion a long time ago, even before Emma. 'So many children. So much pain.'

She pulls back from his, readying herself to walk away again. 'I should be going.'

Jon nods and she walks away, casting a single glance over her shoulder. He watches her leave, then something forces him to set off after her.

'Wait,' he calls out, and she stops.

'Yes?'

'Please don't,' begs Jon. 'Go, I mean.'

The force of the plea holds her in place like a tractor beam. They look into each other's eyes and each sees something of themselves there, the heartache reflected back.

'Would you like a cup of coffee?' he asks her and immediately wishes he hadn't. What is he, fifteen or something?

She bites her lip, then says, 'I'm not sure –'

'I thought we could...talk.' Jon attempts a smile.

'I really shouldn't.'

'Please.' That word again, so small but so powerful. She gives a slight nod of the head. They begin walking together, away from the grave and up along the path. 'My name's Jon, by the way.'

'Abi,' the woman replies.

At first the conversation is awkward and stilted. They sit

opposite each other at a table in a quiet café, the only other people there an old man in the corner reading his newspaper. Abi has been stirring her tea for about five minutes when he breaks the silence.

'Will someone be waiting for you, then?' Once again, it's the kind of thing that's said and you wish you could take it back instantly. Too nosey, too forward.

Abi comes out of her daze. 'Someone... Oh, I see.' She shakes her head. 'You?'

'My wife,' says Jon, then adds quickly, 'ex-wife... Well, she's barely spoken to me since...'

'It happens a lot,' states Abi with all the conviction of one it's happened to. 'All they can see when they look at you is...'

Jon rubs his forehead. 'No, it was my fault, you see. Claire...she was at her sister's for the evening. I should have checked on Em more often. But the monitor was on; I thought it would be all right.'

'What happened?' asks Abi, gazing at him intently.

'Fell asleep, didn't I.' Jon slams his fist on the table. 'Idiot. Fucking idiot!' He draws the attention of the man in the corner and the waitress, but they both look away when he glances up. 'Sorry...'

'No need,' Abi assures him.

Jon breathes out. 'By the time Claire got back...it was too late to do anything.'

'It wasn't your fault.'

Jon jabbed a finger into his chest. 'I was the one looking after her.'

'Yes, but it could have happened anytime. It *does*

happen anytime.' Abi gazed into her still swirling teacup. 'That's what people kept telling me... Took a long time to realise they were right.'

Jon is starting to grasp that they have more in common than he first thought. Not only the end result, but the way.

His voice is softer when he asks, 'Joshua?'

Abi nods sombrely. 'Tuesday afternoon. 2 o'clock to be precise; God, look, I even know the exact time.'

Jon wishes he even had that. But all he has is a rough estimate.

'Joshua was having a nap but...but he never woke up.'

'And since then you've blamed yourself, haven't you.'

'There was no-one else *to* blame,' she snaps. 'Mark wasn't even home. He couldn't understand... No one can.' Abi cries, the tears running a race down opposite cheeks. Instinctively, Jon reaches out and takes her hand. He squeezes it.

'Not true.'

Abi looks at him, her mascara a mess, then she pulls her hand free.

'I have to go.'

'Abi...'

She rises swiftly. 'Thanks for the coffee, Jon.' But before he can stop her she is out of the door, out of his life again. Jon slumps back into his seat and sighs heavily.

✳

Another day, and he is at the graveyard again. The sky is grey, there's little trace of the sun. If he's honest with himself, he's been coming here the past few days as much in the hope of seeing Abi again as to visit Emma, though he's loathe to admit it to himself. But she never returned.

Out of curiosity, Jon finds himself at Joshua's grave today. To all intents and purposes, it is just the same as all the others, but the words on the inscription mean something now that he has met Abi: 'Joshua Hill, Now at Peace.'

He hears the clacking of heeled boots behind him, then Abi's voice: 'I can remember the day Joshua was born.' He doesn't turn, partly because he doesn't want to scare her off again, partly because he wants to hear this. 'Mark was there holding my hand, and his face... I don't think anything could have upset him at that moment. We were a family and...and now, now it's all gone.'

When he hears her sobs, Jon has to look around. They're wracking her body, she's almost hunched over with them. He reaches out a hesitant hand, then decides to just put his arms around her. She doesn't resist, but holds onto him like a shipwrecked sailor might cling to a rock.

'Why did this have to happen to us, Jon? Why is life like this...?'

'I don't know,' he says honestly.

A chill wind blows through them and Abi shivers.

'Come on, let's get you out of the cold.' Jon puts an arm around her and walks her up towards the park.

The sound of the windchimes jangling follows them – but one in particular, one louder than the rest.

Jon and Abi sit at the kitchen table, the half-empty bottle of Brandy between them, the rest of the space being taken up by papers scattered over the surface. Abi still has her coat on; she is looking around at the state of Jon's kitchen.

'I'm sorry about the... What can I say, I'm a pig.'

'I've seen worse.' Abi picks up a manuscript from the table, examining it. Jon takes it off her and tosses it aside. 'Is that what you do, write?'

Jon laughs. 'I *read*, believe it or not. For a publishing house.'

'Sounds interesting.'

'It really isn't. They send me all these cheesy romance books. You should see some of it, things that would never happen in a million years.' Jon takes a swig of his drink.

'It won't help,' she tells him.

'I know, but it dulls the pain for a while.'

'Only for a while.'

Jon ignores the last comment. 'C'mon, drink. It'll do you good.'

Abi takes a sip from the mug in front of her. 'But it won't bring them back.'

'Nothing ever will.'

This time it is Abi who reaches across and takes Jon's hand. He looks up, surprised and she gives him the closest thing to a smile he's seen on her lips.

'I think I'd better be going,' she tells him, getting to her feet.

'So soon?'

Abi nods. 'But I'll see you again. I'm not that hard to find.' She walks around the table and kisses him on the cheek. 'Thank you.'

'For what?'

'For listening. For understanding.'

Then she is gone again. He hears the slam of the front door. Jon brings the cup to his lips, his hand hovering there. But he doesn't drink. In fact he places it back down on the table again.

And it begins from there.

The more he sees of her, the more he wants to. Jon takes her to the café, they walk through the park together, have dinner at Jon's flat – which he makes the effort of cleaning, just for her. They talk, and they talk. If he'd read it in one of the novels they were still sending him to work on, he would have dismissed it as unbelievable, yet this is his life now, as real as anything he's ever experienced, the joy or the pain.

Jon barely notices the passing of the months, but the length of the grass and the flowers in bloom rather than just on the graves tell him it is spring; a time for new beginnings. Even the tree above Emma's grave is now in full leaf.

As they stand there together he ventures, 'Abi?'

'Yes?'

'Something's been worrying me...'

She looks scared, frightened of what he might say next. 'What is it?'

'Do you ever wonder if what we're doing is wrong?'

'Wrong, how?'

He shakes his head, not sure how to explain. 'I don't know. It's just...these past few months, with you. I'm starting to feel things I really shouldn't. I'm starting to feel happy again and I don't know if I have the right.'

Abi touches his face. 'What happened was terrible. There isn't a day goes by when I don't wish I could see Joshua again... But how long can we go on punishing ourselves, Jon?'

'I just can't help thinking –'

'I know...' she leans in close to him. 'But the alternative scares me so much more. I...I don't want to lose you as well.'

Then she kisses him softly on the lips. When she pulls away, he promises, 'You won't.'

That night they make love, their movements slow and loving, comforting even. Outside, the gusts of wind rise and fall to the rhythm of their bodies. And when the release comes it's like they've both been waiting for this since their individual tragedies.

And in the distance, though neither of them can hear it, comes the sound of a distinctive jangling.

Jon is reading through one of the manuscripts when Abi knocks on the door to his flat.

She's almost hysterical, and he can't make out what she's trying to say at first. Then he hears the word 'late' and it hits him all at once.

'There's no doubt?'

'I took a test...' Abi informs him. 'And even if I hadn't I've been throwing up in the mornings... What are we going to do? Jon, I'm scared.'

He holds her, feels her trembling. 'Shh. Don't, love. It's going to be okay. Really, it's all going to be okay.'

Jon starts to tremble too.

It all happens so quickly.

Suddenly they are looking at bigger places, discussing mortgages. Abi puts her house on the market, but there's still nothing in their price range without putting themselves in debt. It's worth it, though, when they see the perfect home; in a nice little neighbourhood, down a cul-de-sac, away from everything.

They marry at the registry office, honeymoon at the coast.

Abi swells up like a balloon, gets heartburn most

nights and her back aches, but Jon rubs it for her. Neither of them talks about the future, only the here and now. That's all that counts.

Their son is born in the early hours of the morning at The Royal Hospital in the centre of town. There are no complications and the baby is healthy.

'We have a son, Abi,' says Jon as the baby is handed over to Abi.

'Do you have any thoughts about a name?' asks the midwife.

'Yes... Yes, we're going to call him after his father. Jonathan.' She smiles.

'Jonathan Joshua,' corrects Jon, before kissing her, then the newborn child. A photograph is taken to mark the occasion.

Jon stands in front of his daughter's grave. He has brought more orange and yellow flowers which he places on the mound. A peace offering more than anything.

'I know I haven't been around as much as I used to be. I'm sorry. But Em, you have a little baby brother. His name's Jonathan. J.J. And I, well, I just wanted you to know that I won't be making the same mistakes with him as I did with you. Besides, he's got you to watch over him, hasn't he.'

The windchime above begins to jangle and Jon looks up, cocking his head. 'Emma?' The windchime jangles more loudly now, then suddenly falls silent. Jon opens his mouth to speak, staring upwards. He lets his head fall and walks away.

If he'd looked more closely, he would have seen that the angel now had its hands covering its eyes.

Jon lets himself into his house with a key and steps into the hallway.

'Abi? Abi, are you there, sweetheart?'

He takes a look in the living room, but there's no-one there. His eyes fall on the framed picture, on the table next to the chair. It shows him, Abi and Jonathan together after the birth. Then he spots the clock. It's 2 pm.

A strange feeling hits him, like an icy wind – Jon shivers. 'Abi...Abi?'

Climbing the stairs two at a time, he makes for the bedroom. Opening the door, he sees his son laying by the window in his cot. He isn't making any noise, isn't moving in fact. He rushes over, bends, but can't hear any breathing, no breath except his own.

'Jon...' The voice behind him. He spins around.

'Abi...quick, call for an ambulance. Jonathan –'

'Jon, it's better this way...Better than waiting for it to happen again,' she tells him. And there's something about her face, an odd glint in her eye. 'Now he'll be at peace. Now he'll be with Joshua, with Emma.'

Jon can't quite take in what he's hearing. He grabs Abi by the wrists. 'What have you done? WHAT HAVE YOU DONE?'

But she doesn't answer him. Doesn't speak again. Not even when he shakes her. Not even when the police and the ambulance arrive.

It's dark and Jon watches her being taken away. He sits on the steps, head in his hands. Someone puts a blanket around him because of the chill.

He feels numb. Dead inside.

Sunday morning and the city is asleep.

The trees are completely bare and Jon is standing in front of another grave, next to Emma's. He is wearing a dark coat, dark glasses.

The inscription reads: 'Jonathan Joshua Cassidy – J.J. Taken before his time. He will speak to us on the wind.'

Jon lays down another bunch of flowers. 'I'm sorry...' he says, voice wavering. 'Daddy's so sorry. I should have listened...'

He looks up to the branch to the second windchime, a second cherub, placed next to Emma's. He pulls up his coat as the wind begins to rise.

Then he makes his way down the path towards the park, the sound faint behind him of two windchimes, jangling in perfect unison.

Coming to a Close

Aurelio Rico Lopez III

Dee sat inside the parked Civic and watched the fat man enter the house on Delgado. She leaned over to the glove compartment and opened it. The Beretta glinted in the wan light. She took the gun and placed it in her bag.

She waited a few minutes then opened the door and stepped into the street where a cool breeze brushed against her. Even with a coat she shivered, but it had little to do with the wind. It was the chill of anticipation. Things were finally coming to a close.

She looked up and down the empty street. It was late. Somewhere, a TV blared. Someone probably watching Leno. In the distance a dog howled. Casually, she walked towards the house. Thoughts of the past surfaced.

She had been sixteen, walking home from school, when a van pulled up beside her. Suddenly, the door slid open, and two men in ski masks grabbed her and pulled her inside. As the van screeched away from the kerb, a hand clamped a moist rag over her mouth and nose. Dee felt light-headed and passed out. It had happened so quickly, she hadn't even had time to scream.

She didn't know how long she'd been unconscious. When she came to, she thought she had gone blind until she realised she was blindfolded. She tried to cry out for help but she was gagged as well.

Then she felt the searing pain between her legs and the heavy weight over her; a man grunting and thrusting. She struggled, but hands held her down. Dee felt his hot breath on her neck as she writhed under him. She smelled the sickening scent of sweat and alcohol.

The pain! God, the pain... Why were they doing this to her?

Suddenly, the man on top of her groaned and shuddered. Over her eyes, the blindfold soaked with her tears.

The hands that restrained her released. Were they letting her go?

To her left, a voice spoke.

'My turn.'

The sound of chuckles. Three of them.

It lasted an eternity. Dee had drifted in and out of consciousness. When they were finally done with her, they tossed her out of the van. Discarded her like trash. Ashamed and sore all over, she choked on sobs and threw up on the street.

Eight years had passed since the incident. Dee had never returned home. She knew she wouldn't be able to bear the look on her mom's face if she told her what had happened. She felt ashamed and filthy.

Dee raised herself. She had a few boyfriends – that's what she called them anyway. Bikers, drunks, junkies. All losers. But one guy, Robert, had taught her about guns. Even took her firing a couple of times. She got pretty good. Damn good.

She resisted the urge to run to the house. She didn't want to call unnecessary attention to herself. Even though it was late, you never knew when a neighbour might be looking out a window.

Even in the moonlight, the house was a mess. The paint was peeling in several areas, and weeds grew rampant on the lawn.

Dee had dealt with two of the men who had raped her. Two out of three. One more to go. They hadn't seen it coming, didn't know she'd be back. They were too drunk, too high on fucking pussy to notice that the blindfold had come loose.

Dee hadn't forgotten their faces. She never would.

One more to go.

She walked to the door and unzipped her bag. Her fingers curled around the cool steel of the gun.

She knocked on the door. Three hard raps. She waited a few seconds and knocked again.

Little pig, little pig, let me in.

'Coming!' a voice grumbled from inside the house.

The hard click of a deadbolt. The door swung open.

It had been eight years since Dee had last seen this monster. He had really let himself go. He had grown a massive potbelly and badly needed a shave. He held a can of beer in one hand. The man stared, almost recognizing the woman at his door.

'Yes?'

When news of her mother's death reached her, Dee had known it was finally time to come home. She smiled and raised the gun to the man's face. 'Hello, Daddy.'

The Pain of Others

David Wesley Hill

I went down to the basement and pulled Sam out of the dryer. He was giggling. He enjoys tumbling in that machine. I singed my fingers on his hair while dragging him through the small round opening.

'What you want, Frank?' Sam asked. He's not much taller than my knee and his eyes are the shape and color of egg yolks and his lips stretch right out of sight on either side of his face. Maybe it's because his mouth is so large that he can imitate any voice he hears.

'You know the Hansens?'

'I've seen them. Mr. and Mrs. and their boy, Erik. They've got a dog, too.'

'That's them. Well, they're going to Florida for a couple of weeks. Except for Ralph. The dog. They asked Barry Ost to look after Ralph.'

Sam bounced up and down at this news. 'I get it. I get it. Who do you want me to be, Frank?'

'Probably Mr. Hansen.'

'I can do that. I've heard him lots of times. We'll have

fun, won't we, Frank? Lots of fun.'

Sam was so excited that he didn't return to the dryer right away but instead started chasing rats. He's pretty quick and already had one in his fist before I was halfway up the stairs.

Sam isn't very bright but he can read a little so I wrote out a script for him to follow. Then I went to the living room. Dad was sitting on the couch with a rocks glass of vodka in one hand and the remote in the other. He had stripped down to an undershirt and boxer shorts like he does every evening. Both his legs were pale and hairy but the right one was shrivelled and half the thickness of the other and the toes were crimped together. Dad tells people who ask about his limp that he had polio when he was a kid. This isn't the truth. His leg has always been like that. He was watching the news but lowered the volume so I could read him what I had written.

'I like it,' he said. 'When are you going to make the call?'

'The Hansens are leaving early. I'll phone Barry in the afternoon.'

'Sounds about right. Say, you know where your mother is?'

'She told Courtney not to expect her until late. Didn't mention why.'

'What are we supposed to do about dinner?'

'There's leftover Chinese in the refrigerator.'

I went out onto the porch and settled into one of the white plastic chairs and watched cars go by. I was bored. I'm always bored. Sometimes it seems like I've been bored for hundreds of years. All my life.

Mom came home not long after dark and sat beside me. The neighbourhood was hushed and this allowed us to hear distinctly the rhythmic sound of sex coming from the living room behind us.

'You'd think they'd get tired of that,' Mom said.

The next afternoon Courtney and I brought the phone down into the basement. Sam's lips moved while he read the script I'd prepared. 'I can do this,' he said, 'No problem, Frank.' I dialled the number for him since he doesn't have real fingers and held the phone to his ear.

'Barry,' he said in perfect imitation of Mr. Hansen's voice, 'Joe Hansen here. No, nothing's the matter. But we won't be needing you to look after Ralph after all. No, no, nothing like that. We're having him taken to a kennel. Beverly just decided she'd feel better knowing the old boy will receive professional care. Don't worry about the mail, either. We've made other arrangements.' Sam was giggling the moment I switched off the phone.

'I did good, didn't I?' he said. 'Real good.'

We were sitting on the linoleum tiling with our backs against the washer and dryer. Much of the basement was finished but the far end was bare concrete and dirt. That area was littered with old bones and droppings and in one corner was the mouth of a tunnel that Sam had scrabbled out by hand through years of effort. Ten feet past the entrance the tunnel divided. One branch led to the basements of houses all across the neighbourhood. The other wound deep into the dark beneath the ground. Only Sam knew exactly where it led.

Courtney was chewing gum. She blew a large bubble and said, 'When do you think we should check on Ralph?'

'The day after tomorrow,' I answered. 'Or the day after that. They probably left enough food for that long.'

'And water,' Sam piped up. 'Don't forget water.'

'And water,' I said.

The Hansens lived in a Cape Cod, set back twenty yards from the street behind a screen of pine. The mailbox was at the head of the driveway. Courtney and I removed the letters and brochures that had accumulated and piled them neatly to one side of the door. It was past midnight and there was no moon but this made little difference to us and we could see clearly through the windows into the house. Ralph was a mixed breed and not a large dog. He was five years old. He knew that Courtney and I were there and he stood up on his hind legs and placed his front paws on the windowsill in order to return our stare. Through the kitchen window we saw that his food and his water dishes were overturned and empty. He'd made messes on the floor since he hadn't been walked.

'He's getting hungry,' Courtney said.

'Just a little. He's been well fed.'

Ralph began barking. It was only a warning bark and not yet a desperate one.

'Be quiet,' I told him. 'No one can hear you.'

We visited the following night and the night after. Each time we found further evidence that hunger and thirst were beginning to affect Ralph. He was a smart dog and understood that the refrigerator held food. But he wasn't smart enough to open the door himself, although scratch marks in the enamel indicated that he'd tried. Somehow he'd gotten into the pantry closet and tumbled cans around the kitchen. He'd chewed the labels into paste but hadn't managed to get his teeth through the metal of the cans.

Once again Ralph peered out at us through the window. He couldn't understand why the Hansens had left him behind and why they weren't feeding him. Nothing hurts worse than being betrayed by those you love. I looked directly into his eyes and saw in them a lot of anger and a little fear and the beginning of insanity. That's what I like best. Most people assume animals don't have awareness of their own mortality but this isn't the case. They are as knowledgeable of death as any man or woman. They just can't talk about it.

We returned to our own house and Courtney went

downstairs to fetch Sam while I sat on the couch beside Dad. Mom was across from us in the easy chair reading a supermarket tabloid. Courtney placed Sam on the coffee table while I dialled the motel the Hansens were staying at in Fort Lauderdale.

'Hello?' Sam said in an adolescent voice. 'Mrs. Hansen? It's Barry Ost. No, no problem, I just wanted to let you know how Ralph is doing, that's all. He's a good dog. Yes, he's been minding me. But he misses his family, though, I can tell. What? No, his appetite is OK, it's only he looks sort of sad. All right. Sure, I'll be glad to let him run around a little extra.'

I switched off the phone and Sam began bouncing up and down on the table top and scattering knickknacks everywhere. 'I like this,' he said. 'I like this a lot.' He leaped on Courtney and pumped against her jeans until she unzipped the fly and slipped the pants down.

'How long do you think it will take for the dog to die?' Mom asked.

Ralph no longer barked. His muzzle was caked with dried blood from attempts at battering through the doors and windows of the house. He had eaten his own excrement off the floor. We stared at each other for hours through the glass pane separating us. Madness glazed his eyes. Madness and something else. Something I can never own myself but can only borrow temporarily in the pain of others. After all these centuries I still can't put a name to it. But for the time being, I wasn't bored.

'Sam,' I said. 'Go find a rat.'

'Will do, Frank,' he answered. In the darkness his yellow eyes were luminous. 'Then what? What's next?'

'Let it go in the Hansen's kitchen.'

'I get you, Frank. No problem.'

A quarter hour later Ralph's ears twitched. Sam had come up from his tunnel into the basement and opened the door just enough to let the rat through. It saw the dog and scurried away but Ralph was faster. His teeth closed around its neck before it could squeal. Ralph ate the rat in three hurried gulps. I calculated there was enough meat and juice in the rodent to keep the dog alive another day or so without taking the edge off his hunger and thirst. I didn't want him too weak. And now he knew how to kill.

The Hansens were due home from Florida on Saturday morning. Dad and I set up our telescope at the living room window with one end poking through the drawn curtains. I focused it on the Hansens' front door and coupled a video recorder to the eyepiece. I also connected the recorder to the television so that we could all watch.

'They're here,' Courtney said. Mom switched the TV from a cartoon channel to the video feed. Dad refilled his glass with vodka and sat next to her on the couch while Sam and Courtney squeezed in on either side. The telescope had a clear view of the Hansens getting out of their station wagon. They were tanned and looked rested. Mrs. Hansen unlocked the front door and entered the house. We could hear her screaming despite the distance. She staggered back and stumbled to the ground with Ralph at her throat. Mr. Hansen kicked at the dog but that only encouraged Ralph to attack him, too.

'Now, Frank?' Sam asked. 'Is it time yet?'

'Another minute,' I replied. 'No hurry.'

Erik tried to wrestle the dog off his father but Ralph lacerated his arm and he staggered away without having accomplished much of anything. Mrs. Hansen died. I took Dad's pistol and ran outside. Ralph was busy chewing on Mr. Hansen and he didn't notice my arrival until I was squatting before him and we were eye to eye. Ralph knew who I was. He hated me. But by now he was insane with grief and rage and he hated himself as much as he hated the owners who had left him alone to starve. Ralph wanted to die. Instead I crippled him. He lay there an hour until a patrolman thought to use the humane killer.

No one understood why Barry Ost didn't feed Ralph or believed his explanation that Mr. Hansen phoned to say his services weren't needed. Particularly in light of his call to Fort Lauderdale.

Since he was underage, however, he only served a year in juvenile detention. The civil suit against his parents for wrongful death is ongoing. For a month we watched the video every night after the evening news while sharing a bowl of popcorn.

'I like it, Frank,' Sam repeated. 'It's my favourite.'

Courtney blew a bubble until it burst loudly.

Personally I best remember the look in Ralph's eyes as he lay paralysed. For a while it was as if I was alive myself although that, of course, is forever beyond me. Eventually repetition sapped our interest in the video and we placed the tape in the closet along with the others. I was bored again.

I'm sitting here on the porch with Mom and we can hear Courtney and Dad and Sam grunting. Maybe I'll join them. It's something to do.